DONALD SMITH was born in Glasgow [...]
Glasgow and Stirling, he began worl [...]
manager, becoming Director of the Net[...]
has written, directed or produced over f[...]
of the National Theatre of Scotland.

Influenced by Hamish Henderson, Donald was also the moving spirit
behind the new Scottish Storytelling Centre of which he is the first Director.
One of Scotland's leading storytellers, he has produced a series of books on
Scottish narrative, including *Storytelling Scotland: A Nation in Narrative,
Celtic Travellers*, and a poetry collection, *A Long Stride Shortens the Road:
Poems of Scotland*. *The English Spy*, his first novel, is set in the closes,
courts and wynds of Edinburgh, the first UNESCO City of Literature.

Praise for *The English Spy*

*...the plot, pace and moral messages of the unfolding drama will reso-
nate with 21st century readers who will find it difficult to not read this
compelling novel from start to finish in a single session. Engaging from
the opening sentence to the last word, Smith has crafted a novel which
captures the essence of Edinburgh during one of its most colourful chap-
ters in history.* LIFE AND WORK

*Smith does a thoroughly good job of conjuring up the Edinburgh of
1706 and the wheedling, dealing and politicking that went on to get the
Union through the Scottish parliament... Smith's version of Defoe picks
his way through it all, arguing, wheedling, scribbling, bribing and cajol-
ing the cast of nicely-drawn characters. Anyone interested in the months
that saw the birth of modern Britain should enjoy this book.*
THE SUNDAY HERALD

*In charge of the storytelling centre on the Royal Mile in Edinburgh,
Donald has a legitimate claim to be one of the best placed and most
qualified people to write such a book, as the centre adjoins the old lodging house where Defoe lived during his trouble-stirring time in Edinburgh.* THE DUNDEE COURIER

The English Spy

DONALD SMITH

Luath Press Limited

EDINBURGH

www.luath.co.uk

First published 2007
Reprinted 2008

ISBN (10): 1-905222-82-3
ISBN (13): 978-1-9-0522282-7

The paper used in this book is recyclable.
It is made from low chlorine pulps produced in a low energy, low emission
manner from renewable forests.

Printed and bound by CPI Mackays, Chatham

Typeset in 11 point Sabon

Acknowledgements

Before Edinburgh received the accolade of becoming the first UNESCO City of Literature in 2004, it was already a seedbed of literary talent. Ideas and texts were shared, discussed and debated, and advice sought and received, through supportive public and informal networks.

I want to thank Paul Scott and George Rosie for whetting my interest in Defoe, Tessa Ransford and Donald Campbell for encouraging me as a writer, and Stewart Conn and Jennie Renton for giving me invaluable comment on early drafts of this book. They are the real stuff of which literary cities are made.

I must also thank my wife Alison who, years ago, suggested that I write a novel, as play after play went over the top into the slough of neglect into which literary drama normally sinks. The end result, of course, can be blamed on no-one but myself.

A Warning to the Reader

IN 1706 SCOTLAND shared a Queen with England, Ireland and Wales, but still had its own sovereign parliament in Edinburgh. It was eighteen years since James VII and II had been overthrown in a revolution, and within the next ten years there would be three attempts at armed revolt in Scotland culminating in the nearly successful Jacobite Rising of 1715.

In that same year of 1706 a journalist, recently imprisoned pamphleteer and failed merchant, Daniel Defoe, came to Scotland under secret instructions from the English Government. His mission was to persuade the Scots to give up their independence, and he was required to provide London with clandestine reports on affairs in the north.

Although most English people had no wish to unite with Scotland, it was felt vital to ensure the succession of one Protestant ruler for the united kingdoms of Britain and Ireland, Queen Anne being childless and ailing. The Scottish Government led by the Marquis of Queensberry favoured union with England, but there was clamorous patriotic opposition fronted by the Duke of Hamilton.

All of this took place many years before Defoe became famous as the author of *Robinson Crusoe* and *Moll Flanders*. In Scotland he was playing a bewildering number of roles, while still adhering to his Puritan faith and claiming the high ground of political principle. Having worked undercover, he even had the cheek to publish an 'official' history of the Union.

Who was Daniel Defoe? In the end he himself turned to autobiographical fictions to try and find out. The seeds of that late harvest, though, were sown in Edinburgh – making the English novel an early fruit of Union?

Yet why did Scotland surrender its hard won and long cherished independence? The historians remain divided. What is offered here is fiction, yet as Defoe himself shows, the truths or apparent deceits of fiction may be uncomfortably closer to home.

Reader, you have been warned.

PART ONE

GOD MADE ME a scribbler for his own inscrutable purpose. He plucked me from the debtors' jail and placed me in his debt. My writing had not gone unnoticed or unpunished – it put me in the stocks. But now my talents were to be applied to my master's purpose – his political purpose.

I had no other option than to obey. Yet this chimed with my own conviction. To go to Scotland and secure the unity of a new Protestant nation was a spur to my settled inclination, and also a confirmation of my vocation. But that only became clear much later. How long already I had languished awaiting such direction. I travelled north incognito yet brimming with hope and righteous energy. I was innocent of what lay ahead.

Now my book is published, my safe haven is reached. the *History* of the Union between England and Scotland by Daniel Defoe. I added the 'de' in deference to my French forebears. Would that I could dedicate that volume to my patron and protector Robert Harley, but our connection must remain undisclosed.

For the first time you have had an account of these proceedings – the great affair of North Britain. Yet I freely own the whole has not been revealed. My true part lies still in obscurity. The secret history of how Great Britain was made.

Good Mrs Rankin has written from Edinburgh to commend my poor efforts. Propriety, the most important thing, she avers, has been observed. A respectable widow has been allowed to live in peace and pursue her business. I can hear the firm Scots tones of my dear friend. But at times we were storm-tossed and close to shipwreck. That chapter is closed, to our mutual gain in the end, yours and mine.

Yet Isobel may have given me the opening I desire.

What, after all, are our own lives, except a kind of story?

When she gave me her confidence I was moved, for her and for the orphan she had taken to her breast. I felt strangely possessed by their experience even though they were of the gentler sex. My sympathies were aroused and so I believe would be those of any manly reader. That is why I have written this private memoir, as if it were a fiction. You alone must judge who is the author and who a mere actor.

I fear it is like playing God.

๛ ๛ ๛

You cannot understand this story without picturing the town of Edinburgh. Nowhere in Europe, including London, has built higher. The tenements are piled up six or seven stories on each side of the High Street, but clambering also in subterranean layers down through the rocky steeps of the town, north and south.

Descending from the rugged looming fortress on the Castle Rock you follow the stony backbone of the Royal Mile. Halfway to Holyrood Palace, you reach the Netherbow, principal Port or Gate of the old city. Beyond, they say, lies the world's end, wolves and the English. In truth beyond the gate the mansions of Scotland's powerful line the Canongate, forming a ceremonial way to the seat of royal power. Until, that is, Scotland's kings moved to Whitehall and to Greenwich.

Around the Netherbow are bunched ancient medieval lands or tenements. With their twisting turnpikes, forestairs from the street, jutting timbered galleries, shuttered windows and carved stone facades, these buildings were once the lairs of merchants, courtiers and kings. But now they have been layered into urban lodgings, sedimented strata for the often less than great who pack this crag-constricted Scottish burgh. Edinburgh clutches status to itself like a tattered standard.

Mr Foe's lodgings were adjacent to the Port, three storeys up. The narrow turnpike stair was dim and reeking of the ordure in the open causeway. But the room was warm, wood-panelled and open to the street, a snug cabin with easy access to the bridge.

'I hope the room is suitable.'

'It is ideal, Mrs Rankin.'

'As soon as you are ready, come down and take a refreshment.'

'Thank you. I shall.'

Half an hour later, having left his bags securely strapped Foe descended carefully to his landlady's hospitable parlour. Kists, rugs, carved settles, painted beams and a faded though elaborate tapestry populated a room more spacious than his own private chamber. A cheerful coal fire burned in the hearth, drawing the room into itself away from the dirt and noise beyond.

'A glass of claret, Mr Foe?'

'I will, though I am more used to a jug of ale.'

'What you Englishmen call ale is not what we describe as beer.'

'Indeed not. Your ale, Mrs Rankin, is really small beer. A different brew altogether. You might drink a pint or two with equanimity.'

'The Scots, Mr Foe, drink a pint or two of anything with equanimity.'

'Surely sobriety is the rule in Edinburgh. Dissipation is a London fashion. I know that I will find much to admire in the capital of Presbyterianism.'

Sitting on opposite sides of the generous fire, the English visitor and his Scottish host sipped their claret from long-stemmed glasses that glinted in the flickering light of the flames. Foe was small in stature with a stomach spread by early middle age. Beneath an orderly, curling wig his features were precise and neat. A tailored coat and waistcoat bespoke careful preparation, with a dash of fussy self-importance.

'Your business may bring you into closer acquaintance with our ways,' observed Mrs Rankin. 'I believe you have never been in Scotland before.'

Foe looked with interest at the small, well-formed figure on the other side of the fire. A plain yet handsome dress could not conceal the rounded fullness beneath.

'My business here is private. Affairs of trade are uneasy due to the Union question and I am pledged to promote good relations.'

'I keep a quiet house, Mr Foe, which is why my guests find this such a convenient lodging.'

'Guests?'

'Lady O'Kelly arrived today from Ireland. She went immediately to her room to rest.' Foe tugged at his waistcoat. 'She has had a long journey but I sent the lassie to ask her down,' Mrs Rankin continued. 'A refreshing glass will soon restore her colour. This will be her now.'

Dear Nellie,

You can see it just as I talk. As Mr Foe rose, quite the gentleman, in walked Catherine. Yes, Lady O'Kelly is our Catherine got up like a lady of fashion. Those clothes came dear and, being in trade, I could see Foe was impressed. She never blinked, bold as brass. My mouth must have been hanging open. It was like a stage play, not that we have ever seen one in Edinburgh.

'May I present Lady O'Kelly of Balnacross. Mr Foe, a merchant of London.'

Somehow I got that out and they sat down. Then she, Catherine I mean, interrogated the poor man. His business. His politics. His religion. Foe took it very smooth, almost too smooth I thought, Nellie, and you have a nose for those things. A dissenter, he said, without political conviction; he was here on private business.

Then he asked Lady O'Kelly, our Catherine, why she was in Edinburgh. That brought out the actress along with the hankie. Her husband had died three months ago (you remember Robert, Nellie, who was never a knight that I recall though he pretended to landed connection in Ireland). His only surviving relation had since passed away in Edinburgh and she was now here to settle the estate. Another snuffle.

Mr Foe was solicitous. I offered more refreshment and she downed two drams. Finally he made off to his room. Perhaps he did not like a woman to drink.

'What are you doing here?' I started, 'Is Robert dead?' I couldn't hold back, Nellie, as you may credit. 'You left with a name, an estate, a husband. Why risk that now, with false play acting?'

'I worked hard for these gains,' says she. What a coarse way of speaking! I scolded and then she threw it back in my face. These were her words – and I want you to hear them yourself: 'For all the management you had of me and of women like me, you still cling to society.' I am sure I have it exact. 'Don't pretend to rank and then you will rise. Men of breeding wish to bestow, not to yield. Bedchamber intrigue is the true path to power.'

She always had a sharp tongue, that one. But it is true for all that, and I told her so despite her cleverness. I can't repeat what she said next but it had bailies unbuttoned in High Street closes. Her Irish accent slipped then, Nellie, I can tell you. Our own Scots tongue can be very unbecoming.

At the end it came out. Robert is penniless and in trouble. You know what I mean – kings over the water trouble. Ever a gambler. Now Catherine is trying to recover their situation by getting into even deeper waters.

She asked me right out if I still had a connection with a certain nobleman. Could I arrange for her to meet him? Then she offered me any favour I liked in return. Would you credit it? Who does she think I am?

But, Nellie, the worst is I felt afraid for her. Like some mother sheep that sees her lamb heading for a raging torrent. The years melted away – if I wasn't telling you now I wouldn't have believed it of myself.

When I know any more I will write. Don't mention it to any of our acquaintance. How many people here will remember her? She must remain discreet entirely.

Your own,

Isobel

Pens, paper and ink on the table. Shirts in the – what did she call it – press. Brushes and razor on the shelf. Books, notes and letters – one so far – in the iron-hasped chest padlocked under the bed. Key in pocket.

Foe looked round his room and gave a quick nod of satisfaction. All was snug and trig, protected from the darkness. He could hear a wind picking up outside; perhaps it was raining. Magdalen Chapel was in the Cowgate, somewhere to the south below the High Street.

Treading carefully down the uneven turnpike, he realised that it would be almost impossible to pass Mrs Rankin's first floor rooms without being observed. And sure enough, 'Mind the dark stairs, Mr Foe,' she called, 'I always leave this door ajar to cast some light.'

'Thank you. Good evening.'

The heavy door swung onto the outside stairhead and abruptly Foe commanded a sweeping view of the street. He stood for a second, like a surprised general reviewing his unruly parade. Wagons piled with market wares queuing to manoeuvre through the narrow Port. Horsemen weaving through the melee. Pedestrians, their faces lit by torches, muffled against the noise, the stench and the cold. On each side of the causeway a mass of shadows seemed to be pushing towards the light and then ebbing back.

Foe launched into the throng, gathering his cloak protectively across his face. At the Tron Kirk he noticed an idler dangling a torch.

'Are you a cadie?'

'Na, I'm the toun crier.'

'Will you light me to the Cowgate?'

'Aye.'

The ragged youngster plunged ahead of him down a

steep alley, the pitch dark broken only by his bobbing torch. They issued into a narrower, noisier version of the High Street.

'Whaur noo?'

'Point me towards Magdalen Chapel.'

'It's doon there. Will I tak ye?'

'This is far enough. I'll find my own way from here.'

Having paid his dues, Foe was outside the chapel within a minute. Amidst the crumbling morass, a lop-sided door led into a clutter of lesser buildings leaning on the chapel wall. He lifted the knocker and struck twice.

'You are Daniel Foe?'

'I am.'

Foe was led down a gloomy passage into a cramped chamber, where two black-suited men sat before a meagre fire. One stood up.

'You hae letters o introduction?'

These were roughly opened and scanned.

'Please be seated, Mr Foe.' This from the younger, smoother clergyman on the right. 'You understand that our willingness to meet you implies no sympathy for the interests you may represent.' He was tall and stiff, even when seated.

'Be easy, gentlemen. My friends wish simply to hear your views, and to represent the warm esteem in which they hold the Kirk of Scotland.'

'Are you committed to Christ's true Kirk, Mr Foe?'

'I have suffered for that cause.'

'Mister Foe wis pilloried – fur a poem.' The burlier grey-haired minister relished the smear of poetry.

'I wrote in praise of the dissenting clergy in England, though this was not wholly understood.' Foe exhibited suffering self-righteousness.

'In Scotland we ken whit sufferin as a true Christian signifies.'

'Whom do you represent?' The seated and apparently senior man waved Foe and his own companion onto wooden stools.

'You have my letters of introduction.'

A look passed between the two ministers.

'These are from reputable men of God who have little power in England and less in Scotland,' observed the taller man.

'Yet they desire nothing more than the union of our two Protestant nations.'

'We're no a persecuted remnant, Mr Foe. There is ane Kirk o Scotland and we require oor rights an privileges as the national church,' rejoined the greyhead.

'The Treaty of Union would guarantee those rights.'

'What is your authority for that assurance?'

'The English Government,' asserted Foe.

'Weill, you surprise me.'

'Furthermore there is one advantage that even Dissenters enjoy in England. The advantage of trade. England prospers and the future wealth of Scotland lies in a trading union with her closest neighbour. That could redeem at a stroke all the losses suffered from the Darien expedition.'

'An whit o Scotlan's honour? That'll no be so easily pit richt.'

'For whom do you speak, Mr Foe?'

'I am not at liberty to be so direct.'

'We kin see that fur oorsels.'

'But my friends… your friends, are at the centre of affairs, close to policy,' assuaged Foe.

'If, and I say if, the Church of Scotland were to consider

a Treaty, our General Assembly would insist on a separate Act guaranteeing our position.'

'I can see no difficulty. It could be passed with the Treaty.'

'Make sure your superiors are clear on that point.' The negotiating position was driven home.

'Wioot it we would raise the country agin you.'

'But we are rational men, Mr Foe, of some standing in the Assembly.'

'I do not believe that a separate Act has been considered but it is my place and privilege to advise on these matters. If it can be managed in all our interests, my friends would not be ungrateful.'

'The Kirk maun be guided, though we canna speak fur the Covenanters.'

'Covenanters?'

They had not entered Foe's calculations.

'Aye, no all the brethren are sae docile.'

'The continuing Covenanters, or Cameronians as we say, remain unsatisfied with King William's settlement in 1690.'

'The Covenant wisna mentioned.'

'They remain ready to take up arms, where they are strong in the southwest.'

'Can I meet with the Covenanters?' Foe cut in on their exchange.

'The rule o law barely raxes that faur. We dinna deal wi outlaws.'

'Of course. I shall look into it further,' conceded Foe.

'But we micht drap a hint in the richt lug.'

'You have been of great assistance. Messages can be left for me at the White Horse Inn under the name of Deans.'

The younger minister rose in pious exhortation. 'We

must seek the Lord's will for His people in these troubled times.'

'Our times are in His hand. I will leave ahead to avoid suspicion,' responded Foe. He turned back up the gloomy passage and out into the night.

'He's awa. Whit do you think?'

'He's smooth-tongued onyroads, but he micht be useful. Very useful.'

❧ ❧ ❧

The Journal of Lord Glamis. There – I have committed those words to paper.

It is three days since I denied entry to Father Aeneas. Twice he came back. I had him turned away at the door. From my upstairs chamber I watched him drag his steps up the Canongate.

That beautiful head hung down.

Already I feel his loss. What do I miss most? The lean strong body. The raven black hair. The lowered eyes when he heard my confession. Was it not a sin that the gifts of nature should be so prodigal in a man denied fruits of the flesh?

I should burn this journal daily at the altar. Or after each week. Yet these words demand to be written; they cannot any longer be spoken.

This is what I must not tell anyone except myself. It will not please any reader. God does not spy. He already knows my intent.

When I gave the instruction to refuse Aeneas my door, I knew that the change had begun. This was the commencement.

On the outside I shall remain constant. Speaking. Commanding. Voting. Whoring. But anchors on which I rested are twisting on the sea bed. Shifting. I look for the image of my mother as she was in life but find nothing. Uprooted.

It is not my doing. Darien did this to me. It started where I pledged and lost so much in the swamps of Panama. That was to have been my fortune and Scotland's empire. All gone like the last glint of spirits in a glass. Debts are nothing new to my patrimony. My ancestors lived and died with debt. Yet there was always a King to favour and reward.

Three days I have not prayed. Why confess? I have not held his sacred body between tongue and lips. Too dangerous.

An emissary is expected. The papers must come to me and not pass through another's hands. I kept him as a private secretary.

What will Father Aeneas do? He has so many talents he will not starve, but if he does not return to Europe he could be exposed and hung. No track should lead back to me. I must not acknowledge him in the causeway. Those doleful eyes.

I shall play my part to the close. There has been nothing like this before, since everything is to be lost or gained. Can faith provide for that?

かかか

If Edinburgh has a centre on the long spine from castle to Holyrood, it is at St Giles Church, or Cathedral as some are pleased to name it. The law courts are there, the Parliament House and the Tolbooth prison. Appendages small and large attach themselves to the great rambling church, while from the midst, like a thistle, its tower rises, topped by a flowering crown.

Around the venerable monument every vacant space is jammed with taverns, shops, lean-to booths, and outdoor stalls, while precarious upper galleries lean towards each other above the closes. Amidst the press of business beggars push their needs and between the dogs and chickens less salubrious services are openly sold.

Weaving through the fringes of a milling crowd, Foe came suddenly to the courtyard behind St Giles. He was surprised to see the elegant facade of Parliament Hall. It seemed to him more gracious and pleasing by far than the ancient palace of Westminster. A tense atmosphere of anticipation was apparent as Foe came through the crowded lobby. He eased himself up a packed stair into the public gallery to watch the members file in.

Squeezed precariously on the edge of a bench he could see the debating chamber below become a sea of bobbing wigs as peers, lairds and burgh men ranged along each side. His eye was drawn upwards to a magnificent open-beamed roof, heraldically carved and brilliantly painted, and he sensed what his intellect knew, that Scotland was a historical nation.

At the opposite end of the hall, the officers of state laid out the royal sceptre and Scotland's crown on a broad table. The Chancellor took his place and debate began.

'My Lords and Gentlemen, will His Grace the King's Commissioner please explain to these Estates why he desires so eagerly to give away the freedom of this ancient nation?'

Foe realised that this must be the Earl of Glamis, a powerful noble from the north who was known for his connections with the exiled Stewart kings. The Marquis of Queensberry rose to reply.

'My reasons, sir, for conjoining with England on good terms are, first, that England is a Protestant kingdom. Joining with them secures our religion. Second, England has advantages of trade to give us which no other nation can provide.'

Foe was delighted to hear his own arguments so clearly endorsed. But Glamis returned to the attack.

'Before the Union of the Crowns, the trade of Scotland was considerable. The shire of Fife alone had as many ships as now belong to the whole nation. After that union, they went into decay because our money was spent in England. The furniture for our houses and the best of our clothes and equipage are bought in London. Is this the advantage of trade?'

A murmur of support ran round the benches and was picked up by the gallery. Queensberry ploughed on with his prepared text.

'Third, England has freedom and liberty, and fourth –'

'Freedom for Scotland?' Glamis interjected. 'Our affairs are already managed by the advice of English ministers and the principal offices of the kingdom filled with men who are subservient to London.' The challenger drew himself to his full height amidst the rising clamour, an elegant and forceful figure. 'Such is the power of places and pensions that we appear to the rest of the world more like a conquered province than a free and independent people.'

Queensberry refused to give way to the mounting growls. 'So what does His Lordship opposite suggest? A return to the days of war and pillage? How else can peace be secured for two kingdoms in the same island except by an agreed succession and Treaty of Union?' This was the bone of contention and the dogs pounced on it.

'When was peace ever secured by dictating the Scottish succession from England? When the Maid of Norway was drowned at sea, then England gave us a king and fifty years of war. When Cromwell the regicide gave us succession he abolished our monarchy and our government!'

A storm of indignation now broke on the upper table. But Queensberry, flushed and defiant, threw down his papers.

'My Lord Glamis is turned historian. But his eye is on France where resides a Papish Pretender, filled with treasonable design against Her Sacred Majesty Queen Anne!' The assembly came to its feet.

'Shame! You will withdraw that slur!'

'I withdraw nothing.'

'Then answer for it outside this hall.'

The rest was drowned in a welter of protest and counter-protest and the session broke up in confusion. In the ensuing struggle to leave, Foe nonetheless managed to present his letter to Queensberry.

༚༚༚

Before another week had passed, I was launched out in all directions. My first pamphlet on the Scottish situation was dispatched to London from the White Horse Inn. Soon its account of growing support here for the cause of union would be on the stalls and in the coffee houses. Another tack was needed in Edinburgh. So my paper on the benefits to Scotland of removing trade barriers and custom dues was following its cousin post-haste to London. Printed copies would be returned here for distribution. I could not depend on the Edinburgh trade to print discreetly but they would sell at reasonable profit. What might be the benefits of one unified market?

Detailed instructions, promised on my departure from London, had not yet arrived. My master and protector remained silent; my reports, unanswered. What further actions could I take without my patron's authority? That was not a question on which I could afford to linger.

Communications were established with the ministers of religion. Daily I awaited some kind of indication from the Covenanting party. My letter had been received by Queensberry though as yet there had been no reply. Were his relations with my master sufficiently harmonious to support my mission? Things might develop suddenly and unpredictably. It was essential I remain alert yet I confess impatience had not taken hold. There was too much to see and do in this northern capital. All around its citadel, fields and rigs rolled out a prospect of rural order and peace. To the north the eye is led down to the broad river with its glistening expanse of estuary. To the south, hamlets, farms and fine towered houses spread out towards the hills.

The town itself is set amongst its own amphitheatre of rocky and sylvan peaks – Arthur's Seat, Calton and Corstorphine hills. By day the skies kept fine and clear.

When not on business, I walked out of Edinburgh to admire the view over to Fife or to the Pentland Hills. After all, was I not seeking a site for my new manufactory – salt perhaps, or glass, depending on the terms of trade.

I own too that there were nearer consolations in Edinburgh. Mrs Rankin was proving exceptionally civil. She often entertained and each day at some point she would have me into the parlour to exchange news and share some refreshment. What a warm heart her busy form seemed to contain, and so it proved. For now she dealt discreetly, including me in her genial social round without exposing me to public view.

Especially affecting was her attention to the young widow whom fortune had brought to her door. I often saw her in intimate converse with Lady O'Kelly, her head closely bent to that beautiful, well-born lady, whose own head was bowed in sorrow listening to her confidante.

As a husband and father my better instincts were called into play by these moving scenes. I resolved not only to deepen my acquaintance with the lady of the house, but also to speak to Lady O'Kelly. Was there perhaps some way that I, as a practical man of business, could render assistance? It seemed as if all was not easy, or easily resolved, in her affairs.

Nothing in such behaviour would betray my true purpose. On the contrary, a human touch or two might soften any strangeness. It is the wholly isolated who attract suspicion. Naturally my commerce with the ladies of the house should observe strict propriety. My disguise could not become a form of license, like the degradation of a London playhouse. It was a necessity of my purpose.

᪥᪥᪥

'Will I shave you noo?'

The great man was slumped, contemplating his wigs, his bald forehead mapped with stubble, veins and a scattering of pimples. 'Not yet, William, give me your intelligence first.'

'Twa frae Dublin, yin frae Exeter.' A large glass of claret was deftly set to Harley's hand. 'And the first wurd frae Mr Foe in Edinburra.'

'And what has Foe to say for himself?' The Secretary of State's bloodshot lids flickered in interest.

'He's no quite sure why he's there so he gies you a lang list. Do you want to hear it?'

'Give me, as you say, the gist.'

'Aye, the gist. Weill he's tae inform, tae persuade, an he's tae win roond the meenisters.'

'The meenisters?'

'Aye, the Kirk. If ye rile them ye'll hae the country bizzin like plundert bees.'

'Are the Scots really so pious?' Harley took a long pull at his first drink of the day.

'There's a wheen o Godly, but Scots folk love an argie-bargie. Religion's the best ammunition in ony controversie.'

'So it seems. And Mr Foe's text?'

'Aye weill, he reads you a lesson in statecraft.'

'To what effect?'

'Says you need agents everywhere.'

'A settled intelligence.'

'Aye, tae coort popularity – court favour, ye ken.' Reid was itching to clean up his master's cheeks and scabby pow.

'What's his reasoning?'

'The pooer o public opinion – you need tae ken its colour.'

'He's no fool.' Harley drained his glass.

'He also says ye hae tae lee.'

'To what?'

'Lee. Dissemble.'

'Well there's fresh news. I thought he was a Christian.'

Despite his impatience, Reid paused to assess his master's mood and degree of interest. A stocky grey-haired Lowlander, he had been in Harley's service for more than five years and he liked the job.

'He says a lee's no a sin if it disnae hairm onybody. Ye hae to govern so that aabody thinks ye're oan their side.'

'A distinction worthy of a Scotch Calvinist. But to the point – has he done anything?'

'He's winnin roond the meenisters wi guarantees for the Kirk.'

'In the Treaty of Union?'

'They want a separate Act.'

'Scots Kirks in the English Constitution.'

'Whit next!'

'Anything else?'

'He needs money. He pleads his wife an seiven bairns – he disnae want tae leave them oan your haunds.'

'He needs my patronage.'

'You took him frae the debtors' gaol, Mr Harley.'

'I saw the potential. What is his contact?'

'Name of Goldsmith at the White Hart Inn in the Grassmercat. Shall I send instructions?'

'No. Let him find his own feet.'

'Or dangle.'

'Not in your own bonny Scotland, I trust.'

Reid controlled his features. 'Shall I fetch the razor?'

'Yes, William, you can shave me now. And…' He waved his empty wine glass.

My dear Nellie,

This in a hurry since I am run off my feet. The parliament session goes on and on without a break so everyone is in town. There's been nothing like it since they sailed to Panama, or when King William came from Holland in 1690. Every house in the Canongate is open and every High Street lodging full to bursting. You can imagine the result of that. Anyway it always seems to be feast or famine but now there is a glut.

You know, Nellie, how much I long to give up this grievous trade. When the Duke gave me his favour I thought that I would never have to take another young woman under my wing. But the favours of great men are fickle as I have more cause than most to know. My poor heart. Neither of us has had our due. What can't be mended must be tholed, I hear you say.

The grieving widow is still here. Her affairs are not resolved. I am afraid, Nellie, of the outcome, and of getting too involved. Everything you say about that is right but I cannot send Catherine away. Why, when it is too late, do I find myself invaded by a mother's feelings for I know, Nellie, that is what I am undergoing. Is it not inevitable when you think of all the girls we have looked after and instructed? Tell me if this is straying too far beyond the pale? I wish you were here so that we could draw into the fire and talk it through. I need to clear my own head. Then you could see Catherine for yourself. What a beauty she has turned into, tall and proudly formed. She catches every eye and I have to see her covered before going out. She should have the world at her feet.

But, Nellie, she is not my only long-term lodger. I told you did I not about Daniel Foe. On the very same day as

Catherine blew in from Ireland – or so she said – Mr Foe arrived and took up the first room. He is a merchant of London, here on some trade or business to do with the union, or proposed union. Can you imagine Scotland ruled from London? He is a small man but quite neat and well turned out. We are very civil with each other. No not in that way. There is something mannerly in him that is rare in Scotsmen. I can't quite put my finger on it. As if he is treating you like an equal. No, I can hear you say it, perhaps his flattery is more accomplished. Yes, I do like Mr Foe, Nellie. I can see your look. Yet there is more to Daniel Foe than meets the eye. His affairs are very discreet.

Must go – more footsteps on the stair.

I shall write again when I have any news –

Think kindly of me,

Isobel

Time to set out the game. Review positions and calculate the next moves. I have only you now to play against.

Gains and losses have become equal, in my estimation. If you place all the pieces on the table you can view the position.

London needs a Protestant succession. England may be willing to pay well for that security.

Of course, they might invade, but Scotland is hard to hold by force. Long ago they learned that lesson. Moreover, European wars demand our troops. Would Scottish soldiers remain loyal? So they negotiate, first with government and then with us. What price can I command?

King James has France behind him. He is our rightful king, if Scotland were to rise. But money is scarce, and we are divided by religion. Yet the threat is real. Would Scotland not do well to regain her freedom, before our parliament too is lost? Does St Germain desire our freedom or their power restored in London? So they plot first with us and then with England. What will they offer? When will real negotiations begin?

Timing is all. The sides are ranked. The new messages from France may prove decisive.

There is one uncertain player on the board. King, Castle, Knight? Our greatest noble. In opposition, he claims precedence; with him the government must parley. Who knows where Hamilton's heart is settled, or his mind. The Duke's a spinning top. He could expose us all to ruin, Scotland's ruin, or sell at a commanding price. Is Hamilton blood more royal than mine?

I am not in his confidence – who is? I need Aeneas to be my eyes and ears. He has a gift for winning confidence and trust. After all it is his vocation to be believed. I saw him in the street and hurried by. He did not try to approach me.

Does he have a new patron now? A companion?

The game grows tiresome; there is no pleasure in stalemate. Patience, Glamis. You must not give way to feeling. Await events, seek diversion. That is hard to find in Edinburgh, unless you know where to look. As I do.

࿇ ࿇ ࿇

The street was broader here but pitted and uneven. In the

gathering dark, carriages bumped along the causeway. Catherine and her guide stayed in the shadow of the high walls broken only by imposing gates, that yielded glimpses of the aristocratic facades of the Canongate mansions.

Brought up in Edinburgh, Catherine knew this part of town well. Behind the mansions lay classically ordered gardens and postern gates giving access to discreet paths and alleys. But although all of these town residences inclined towards the palace, she had never entered the Abbey Strand or approached the gates of Holyroodhouse. It had a been a relief, therefore, to make contact with Murray.

All had gone as planned, despite the priest's change in status and the consequent switch of tactics. Once secretary, now painter, Aeneas had delivered Isobel Rankin's note under the guise of presenting his own artistic services. Catherine was impressed by the resourcefulness of this tall stranger with the dark, handsome features.

'Here is the gate,' he said, 'Go straight through the private garden to the door at the foot of Queen Mary's Tower. You can see it there between the trees. Three knocks.'

'Where will you be?'

'I'll not move from inside the gate.'

'I don't know how long this might take.'

'If it takes till dawn, I'll be waiting. Try and leave before it turns light.'

'I'd be missed at the Netherbow.'

'Watch for yourself.'

'And you.'

Catherine slipped across the garden, keeping to the turf-laid paths. In the shadow of the tower, she drew a breath and knocked three times. The door opened.

She followed a silent figure two floors up the twisting stairs onto a small landing and was beckoned into a high-ceilinged, densely furnished chamber. The only light came from embers smouldering in an open fire. Catherine struggled to distinguish between the tall carved chairs and any human figure.

'Your Grace, my Lord of Hamilton, are you there?'

'Please come no further.' A male voice, high pitched and wavering, came from the far side of the room, as if muffled by a screen or curtain. 'Sit here by the hanging where I can hear you without seeing your face.'

Catherine felt her way to a seat in front of a heavy velvet drape. 'Are you indisposed, my Lord?'

'It is essential I can swear that I have not seen you.'

'I am sitting down.'

'Have you the letters?'

'Yes, your Grace, I have a letter from the King of France. But you won't be able to read it.'

'Here.' The curtain twitched and Catherine passed the papers through the gap.

'The King of France has done me great honour in writing. I was always his true servant and that of James Stewart... as I still am.'

She could hear the pages being leaved one behind another. It appeared that Hamilton could talk and read at the same time, or that there was nothing unexpected in the letter.

'There are many in Scotland who want James restored but they will not work together, so I have to be extremely careful. I have kept my position by pitting one faction against another.'

'I am to convey your desires back to the King.'

'Do not attempt to communicate with France while

you are in Edinburgh.' This was peremptory and peevish in tone.

'Any message will go back with me to Ireland and then to France.'

'I need money.'

'For arms?'

'Parliament has changed. The Union government is buying votes with money from London. I will be destroyed if I cannot secure the burgh votes. With them, I can stop the Union.'

This was not the purpose of Catherine's mission. 'King James believes the time is right for a rising,' she suggested.

'What does King James know of Scotland?' Hamilton's voice rose a further notch. 'France may incite us to take up arms, but for them it is only a diversion from the war in Europe.'

'The French will supply what is needed in money, men and weapons.' This was the main point of the letter.

'I believe that this is the moment to shake off the English yoke.' Catherine could hear movement on the other side of the curtain and the voice seemed closer. 'But I doubt if we could undertake to restore King James. Could Scotland conquer England? Yet when Queen Anne dies without an heir it would be easy for us to break with England and choose our own King.'

Catherine was unsure where Hamilton was leading. 'How could you rise without claiming James as your lawful King?'

'That would be the best way. Nothing would be easier than to take control of Scotland. The foolish enthusiasm for London spoils everything. It will be quite soon enough to speak of the form of government or of who is to be

King when we have shaken off the English yoke. Were James a Protestant, there would be no difficulty at all, nor any need for foreign troops.'

'But Scotland has no army.'

'I alone can raise fifteen thousand men, and the rest will follow where I lead. I am of the royal blood. Scotland owes me some allegiance.'

'Your Grace, forgive my questions.' Catherine pulled back from these dangerous revelations. 'I am eager to serve my King. Please accept my humble service.'

The Duke accepted his due readily. 'Of course. Come beside me and we can speak more intimately. You must tell me about life at St Germain.' A gap appeared in the curtain.

'Your Grace does not want to hear my gossip.'

'France is often in my thoughts. I should have had the Duchy of Chatelrault, for it was given to my ancestor in the time of the auld alliance. It would be but fair recompense, since I might lose the revenues of my wife's estate in Lancashire.'

'The King of France will surely recognise your right,' Catherine moved to a soothing tone.

'I am putting everything at risk.'

'You will not put your wife in danger.'

'She has borne me many children but she has a peevish disposition.'

'It must be an effect of childbearing.'

The curtain opened further.

'You cannot blame me for seeking assurances.'

Catherine did not relish receiving further confidences. 'I have come to assure you of support,' she tried. 'All Europe looks to your leadership and valour.'

Hamilton was now fully visible. The long nose

and receding chin seemed to quarrel with each other, undermining his air of command. 'We shall throw off the English yoke. Wait here till daybreak and I will give you a ciphered letter to the King of France.'

'But you will see me in the light of dawn.'

'Lie behind the curtains of my bed. While this is done, I will fetch a light and read you a paper on the claims of my house and blood.' A soft hand drew Catherine in to the enclosing warmth.

'It is quite dark in here, your Grace. Can I remain with safety?'

'You are in my most private apartment.'

This was Catherine's first time in a royal bedchamber and she looked at the hangings with interest. Who had once lain against the pillows?

'I believe that you will appreciate the style of this discourse,' said Hamilton.

�����

Two communications came into my hand, one care of Mr

Deans at the White Horse Inn, the other an official letter from the Marquis of Queensberry addressed to Mr Foe at my lodgings. Holding them tightly together I hurried to my sanctum. This at long last was progress.

The Marquis invited me to counsel a Committee of Parliament established to consider customs duties and trading levies in the event of Union negotiations. It was framed as a reply to the letter of introduction which I had handed him in Parliament the night of the debate.

This was most gratifying, since in truth none was better qualified for this role, given my wide experience of business, commercial and political.

But how did Queensberry know this? My pamphlets were unascribed. Had he taken my recommendations at face value? Was that the way such men of power behaved? Surely my protector had written as Secretary of State to Scotland and Harley's unseen hand, undeclared to me, was guiding my passage even in Edinburgh. That would be reassuring, in the absence of direct instructions.

Yet since my arrival in the north, I had begun to doubt. Did Harley's writ run here as in London? Scotland's rulers had their own design on my efforts. I needed to be closer to Scottish Government were I not to fall between two stools. Now I was summoned to Queensberry's mansion in the Canongate. There I might find out, or be discovered in my turn. I could not turn back now. Attendance on the powerful is always instructive.

The second missive was more oblique. A single sheet without signature or source, it read, 'Colonel Kennedy of Ballintrae. Master of Foils.'

I had not heard of this gentleman. But it seemed that my fencing skills were in need of sharpening. If Kennedy was in Edinburgh, he should not be hard to find through those ubiquitous street boys, the cadies.

I placed both communications in the chest and pushed it back beneath my bed. I felt tension ebb, an easing of the limbs. I stretched out upon the blankets and enjoyed their warmth. I was satisfied that my resolution had been kept intact.

As I relaxed, Lady Catherine came into my mind. Slender, her brow smooth, her black hair uncovered... from her white shoulder a loose mantle began to slide beneath her breasts.

God keep me from such imaginings. What if that grief-stricken and honorable lady could look into my soul. These are offences against virtue, for which I should be judged. I rose quickly, smoothed my garments, and prepared to meet my hostess in her homely parlour.

෩෩෩

'A basin, William, a basin. Hurry.'

Reid had been dozing by the fire. Coming to, he was shocked by the grey waste of his master's face. Harley collapsed into the chair vacated by his servant. 'Pull my boots off.'

Trying to oblige, he tugged hard. 'They're ticht.'

'I know that, man, gently.'

'You're like a lame cuddy.'

'Throw in the salts. Aah.' Two bare contorted feet were submerged in warm water.

'You've had a lang nicht o it.' Reid discreetly removed Harley's wig before it slipped off by its own accord.

'That's better. I can't endure state dinners. You spend most of the time on your feet waiting on Her Majesty's pleasure. The Good Queen Anne.'

'Shall I mix a toddy?' Reid soothed professionally. 'The water's heated.'

'Please, and make one for yourself.'

'As you wish.' It was going to be one of those long evenings.

'Come on. Don't stand on ceremony.' Harley waved expansively round the parlour. 'Can you guess the talk tonight at Court? Scotland, bloody Scotland. Why haven't we concluded the Treaty? Of course, let me dictate a letter now and settle it. Bring pen and paper, man. Can the Scots not be managed?' Reid focused on mixing the whisky, hot water and honey.

'Or why, God help me, am I destroying the English Constitution? How am I destroying this perfect work of creation? By giving the Scots a share of sovereignty. Forgive me, but there is no end to the affair – the longer it runs, the worse it gets. I can't bear to hear anything more about Scotland.'

'They're agin it theirsels, the Scots.'

Harley took his toddy and sucked in thankfully. 'Whisky – a peasant's drink, they say? Nectar of the gods.' For a moment he appeared to subside. 'What is Foe doing up there?'

'He's pit oot some broadsheets.'

'The exiled Stewarts are feted in France, the Spanish are waiting their chance for a Catholic alliance. Scots tinder could set Europe alight. What use are pamphlets?'

'The back door maun be steekit.'

'Or I'll be out of office.'

Reid sipped thoughtfully. 'Ye hae the main men bocht up.'

'A majority in the Scots Parliament is all but assured.'

'Fower, maybe five men hae Scotland in their gift. Nae rebellion can succeed wioot a leader. Are they aa secure?'

'You're right. There may be a weak link. Light candles in the study, William. I will write before I retire. You can take this away now.'

Reid gathered up the basin and towel and left the room.

'It's all a question of the correct treatment at the right time. Bloody feet,' Harley muttered.

෨෨෨

Bright, clear light streamed across the morning town. Where

closes pierced the street line, unexpected sunbathed vistas opened to the hills of Fife. It was another fine autumn day in Edinburgh, defying the southern wisdom that Scotland was always wet and windy, Foe reflected.

He walked up the High Street, past the Tron, to St Giles, where he cast a professional eye around the Tolbooth Jail, stacked like a child's playhouse against the Gothic giant of the medieval Church. Early warmth had brought out the beggars and the hawkers to claim their places in the bustle of the day.

Turning left and then sharp right, he proceeded down the shadowy tunnel of the West Bow, dwarfed by the houses which struggled precariously against the gradient to ascend out from their dark roots into the light. Suddenly emerging into the open sweep of the Grassmarket, he moved across the square and then turned to confront the precipitous wall of buildings on the north side, which merged seamlessly into the sheer rockface of the Castle Craig.

The massive fortress commanded respect. Above the natural rocks, the formidable redoubt of the Half-Moon battery formed an impregnable buttress against allcomers. Again Foe acknowledged the deep historical foundations of this nation, for which destiny intended a new departure. For a man who knew prison from the inside, there was something oppressive in the way this fortified citadel brooded over Scotland's capital. How many poor souls had rotted in its dungeons and how many brave individuals whose only fault was to defy an arbitrary despot had been marched out to be hung or dismembered?

Shrugging off these gloomy reflections, Foe scanned the inns and shops ranged along the edge of the market, which was filling up by the minute. The White Hart was clearly visible. Although it was one of his poste restantes, so far the cadies had called here in vain. Threading his way reluctantly through cattle drovers, wagons and ordure, he picked out a burly figure standing beside the archway into the inn's courtyard. Strength and weight conjoined beneath a plain brown coat, cord breeches and tall military boots.

'Mr Foe.'

'Colonel Kennedy.'

'Of Ballintrae. At your service, sir.'

Kennedy wore his grey-streaked hair tied back in a pigtail. Cold blue eyes met the visitor's enquiring gaze. Foe dipped his head in acknowledgement.

'Well, come through Mr Foe and we'll see what you're made of.'

The archway opened into a small cobbled court which the sun had not reached. Two rapiers leant against a stable door. Kennedy stripped off his coat.

'This is a good quiet spot. No-one overlooks the Hart's backyard except the cannon. You're very short, Mr Foe. Will this blade suit you?'

'It's fine, thank you.' Foe took off his own jacket.

'Right then, let's go through some basic moves. No time like the present.'

The Englishman was careful not to give himself away too soon, but Kennedy quickly gauged that he was no stranger to the art, and began to exercise in earnest.

'Defend, Mr Foe, keep the arm extended. Now, lunge. Aye that's it. On guard. Fence. Parry and lunge.'

'And cut.'

'Good, Mr Foe. Defend.'

Foe was soon out of breath and propped himself against the door.

'You have the better of me, Colonel.'

'It's a game for old hands.'

'But an ancient and honorable game. You'll make a gentleman of me yet.'

'I don't fence for sport. One day you might have to fight for your life, as I have done.' Kennedy pulled on his coat.

'Is duelling not the sport of gentlemen, Colonel?'

'In Scotland everyone has to fight for their own, gentleman or no.'

Foe moved confidentially towards the Colonel's towering bulk. 'I think you understand my business here, Colonel Kennedy. Will you deliver my message?'

'Aye, but they'll not heed you.'

'Why not?'

'Covenanters have no interest in a Kirk that has betrayed their cause.'

'But all Scotland pledged itself to the Covenant.'

'And then forgot it. These are stubborn men, Mr Foe, who remember the blood that flowed out there in the Grassmarket. You would do better to send a sermon.'

'What can be done?'

Kennedy watched him take a disconsolate turn round the yard.

'I might be able to help you.'

'What is your influence?' Foe's sharp features sharpened.

'They look to me because my father was a leader of their cause. And because, like him, I am a soldier.'

'Do they intend a rebellion?'

'Overthrowing tyranny, Mr Foe, is not rebellion but a religious duty – for Covenanters.'

'They do not favour Union.'

'I see you're catching on fast. Yet they'll not want to act like Jacobites or Papists.'

The two men faced each other across the narrow court, calculating how far each might go.

'I might restrain them for a while.'

'If I had your assurance for that effort.'

'It would need more than assurance.'

'I would have to consult my friends before taking it further.'

'Well then, Mr Foe, it seems that you will require more lessons, if your stay is to be extended.'

'I am at your service, Colonel.'

'Excellent, I am sure the host here will fetch up a good bottle of claret. Exercise always works up a thirst.'

Foe winced as a huge hand clapped him on the shoulder and steered him into the inn.

෯෯෯

Re-clothed in his formal dress, the Earl of Glamis was an

imposing and graceful figure, yet his narrow aquiline face denied him the epithet handsome. There was something disconcerting about the way his pale green eyes shifted focus so rapidly. Mrs Rankin did the honours, serving wine personally. Catherine, who had ushered their distinguished visitor back into the parlour, helped herself to a glass. Often, she remembered, with aristocratic clients Isobel would call up the maid. Perhaps this was economy. More likely, discretion.

'Your health, sir. Please take a seat.'

'Thank you.'

Glamis' lips could be seen testing the wine, before drawing the rich liquid into his mouth with lingering pleasure.

'I trust that your visit has been satisfactory.' Mrs Rankin gathered her skirts neatly beneath her as she sat.

'Most pleasurable. I find intimate converse a great relief in these stressful times. It is a pity that such relations could not be extended to public affairs.'

'Even the common people might be won over to such a Union.' Catherine looked Glamis in the eye.

'Many voices are raised in opposition,' Mrs Rankin intervened, disapproving of these courtly indecencies.

'Including that of your delightful new companion, or so she tells me. Where do you come from, my dear?'

'Catherine is an old acquaintance, your lordship. She is known in Edinburgh.'

'I would like to know more. Perhaps I could assist your cause, Catherine? You seem reluctant to confide in me, on first acquaintance.' Glamis smiled thinly.

'You know our conventions, Glamis.' Mrs Rankin was determined to maintain a professional distance. 'Many in Parliament do not favour an English succession.'

'I am, as ever, the true servant of our royal house.'

'Will Parliament vote against negotiations?' asked Catherine, showing her first interest in the conversation.

Glamis waited while his glass was refilled. 'Parliament is sure to vote. Perhaps tomorrow. The English insist on liberality.'

'What if the English don't keep their promises?' observed Mrs Rankin sharply, discomforted by this blatant avowal.

Glamis took a slow sip of wine, leaned back and let his eyes travel over Catherine.

'My dear ladies, Queen Anne's word is her bond, though of course the Queen's ministers may cloud Her Majesty's vision. Duplicity cannot be ruled out. If negotiations go well, I shall have a town house and coach in London. If, however, an English treaty provokes rebellion, I shall raise King James' standard at the head of my worthy kinsmen and tenants. Our loyalty to the Crown is well known.'

'They say that in love the divided heart cannot conquer.'

'And that is why I am so passionately devoted to your beauty, my dear. The white cockade rules in my heart and I must know more about you, or suffer the consequences.'

'Then you must come back and visit us again.' countered the hostess firmly.

'Your discretion, Mrs Rankin, is infallible. I will send you a note, but in the meantime I must go back to Parliament.' Glamis unwound from his chair.

'I hope that the members will remain calm.' The lady of the house came to her feet like a matron admonishing unruly charges. 'These late sittings provoke nights of riot.'

'Parliament is like a London playhouse, full of sound

and fury. I perform, but prefer the quiet of the Green Room.' Glamis brushed Mrs Rankin's hand with his lips.

'You must have it both ways,' she acknowledged.

'I believe I shall. The master must hunt with his pack.'

'What of the hounds and gillies? Does the master spare a thought for them?'

Glamis looked back towards Catherine, who had remained seated as she spoke. 'Why should he – they are born to serve. You have my deepest appreciation. Good day.'

Mrs Rankin followed him to the door and closed it behind him. A faint scent was left in the air between the two women.

'He's gone.' Catherine murmured, relapsing wearily into her seat.

'Aye, licking his lips like a cat that's been at the cream.'

'So I am still an asset to Scotland at least.'

'Why come back to this, Catherine? You were well out of it. Look at him – I could barely keep civil with the leech. God forgive me.' Mrs Rankin resumed her seat and reached for a hankie.

'Don't worry. I'm only trading selectively.'

'Glamis would stick a knife in you as soon as look at you. He thinks people are slaves to be used as he thinks fit, men and women.'

'But he has lots of them, and that makes it important.'

'Whatever your business is here, Catherine, don't deal with Glamis.' Mrs Rankin had abandoned her habitual reserve. 'Women for him are not humans, far less equals. He uses us like animals.'

'Don't, Isobel, please don't be upset.' Catherine reached out a hand to the older woman. 'I haven't come to cause you trouble.'

'Can you not see, lass? I thought you at least had won clear of all this. It breaks my heart to think I set you on this path.'

'My mother was dead and I was deserted by my father, without a friend in this crowded town. You cared for me like a parent.'

'God help us both.'

'I was never free, Isobel, then or since. But now I intend to make my own way, whatever the cost.' Catherine withdrew to the other side of the fire, and the moment of intimacy was lost.

☙☙☙

My dear Nellie,

You must not think of coming to Edinburgh on a visit though you know how I would like to have you here beside me. The mood of the town is ugly and violent. You can feel it in the air. Parliament sits late every night debating the Union question so people refuse to leave the streets until the last moment before the curfew, and even then they are reluctant to withdraw as if without their presence some terrible treachery will take place. The taverns empty and every beggar, pickpocket and street girl hugs the edges of the multitude. Word passes down of some speech in favour of the Union and then anger builds and the mob breaks out. Some say it is all stirred up by the opposition but I am not so sure. It is like a beast crawling from its lair ready to fight to the death.

Do I sound extreme? This language is like Daniel Foe's exaggerations. He is still here describing everything and very talkative after a glass or two of claret. More of that later.

As you know, Nellie, my real concern is our business. Catherine is working again but very strangely. She only converses with a few select gentlemen. I am sure that she did meet with a nobleman of our acquaintance, to what purpose I am ignorant, nor am I likely to be told since God knows she shares few confidences with the woman who was her mother in all but name.

I suppose I should be grateful for what help she offers in this hectic time, but I want her out and away back home for all our sakes. What is this madness that has taken hold here, and as you write in Glasgow? The country has gone clean gyte. Things I believe have never been the same since Darien and 1690 but I must hold my tongue. Whatever, it has all got much much worse.

They say that the Duke could stop the Union.

The patriotic factions look to him. I feel very queasy hearing such talk – you know what I mean, Nellie. Yet it makes me quite proud to think that he could lead affairs, though that would need a moment of decision. Fortunately he is not much in my thoughts. It is almost two years now and Catherine's return would have driven it all from my mind, if she had not harked back to all those things that are better forgotten.

We must manage this discreetly – it is the only way for women to keep some measure of control, for once exposed we are powerless. God keep the girl, though no lassie now. She is a work of nature.

Mr Foe has taken on himself to be very troubled about her. I can see sympathy in his gaze. He would like to help but of course he knows nothing and appears to suspect nothing of our business. Is this likely in such a clever man, but he does believe in Presbyterian virtues and in our adherence here in Edinburgh. I must recommend a stay in Glasgow for his education. Truly he knows everything of history, trade and politics. Foe is a man of the world who is oddly theoretical. Yes, he has a wife and by his own account seven children but, I judge, little knowledge of women. How can I tell? Your speculations, Nellie, are quite unfounded. I am the soul of propriety these days.

I do confess I like him in a fashion. There is something decent and respectful about him, for all that his business here is undeclared. Foe treats you as an equal and asks your views. Most remarkable in a man. He entertains me even when I have to curb my tongue or stop myself from laughing outright. His sincere calling to understand this town and its Scottish ways leaves him floundering. I find it truly comical and most comforting.

Yes, Daniel Foe is interesting and intriguing. He is not telling the whole truth of his affairs, not yet at any rate. I think that may be his step on the stair. I shall try and finish this later, if there is any more to say.

Your dear friend,
Isobel

Who is she? Not one of Rankin's standard whores, high

class as these can be. Known in Edinburgh I doubt. She has the body of a Queen laid down beside me. I did not think my interest would revive so quickly and all at once. A surfeit of politics has made me dull and turgid.

Had Aeneas begun to blunt my appetite and dull the sharp edge of my desire? Yet she reminds me of Aeneas. Her size, and form, and colouring are so like, with only the sex diverging. So noble but so common. What is this mystery of blood?

I saw Aeneas with a canvas under his arm. He must be drawing again. I should command him to paint himself, or the beautiful whore.

I shall go back to the Netherbow, as soon as this tedious business achieves its long drawn out conclusion. How many more hours must I listen to the laird of Saltoun's patriotic sermons, his Scottish republic? Fletcher's rant they call it, and the common folk cheer him on. Even in Parliament we hear the mob baying outside the walls. The Chancellor and all his cronies skulk through the streets for fear of riot and attack.

But Hamilton lies low. The lion in the lair awaits his time. For what? I hold the opposition front and descry negotiation knowing that negotiation is the certain outcome. But who will treat? Who will set out the terms? I should go to London as a Commissioner but not now; things in Edinburgh are too diverting.

Weigh equally, Glamis, and keep all paths open. This debate cannot go on much longer. Please let it reach an end and make some kind of climax.

ॐ ॐ ॐ

Time to take stock. Like any honest tradesman I had to

reckon up the debts and credits of my project. Rumour had it that with another sitting the Scottish Parliament would vote for or against negotiation. I owed it to my patron to reckon up the gains and losses, but I was nervous of the result.

Once a bankrupt, now I was called to give an account of nations. Such is the mystery of providence that even in our guilt we may become instruments of a saving remedy. Our times are in His hand though we cannot see the ends.

Sixteen pamphlets had been written and circulated with what result I did not know. I had been summoned to Queensberry House in the Canongate but the Marquis did not receive me in person. Instead I was commissioned to prepare some papers for the Committee on Customs Duties. So my grasp of necessary detail was acknowledged, but not my influence on affairs.

From Colonel Kennedy there was no word of these sectarian Covenanters. Lord Protector Cromwell had their measure in his day when he left ten thousand corpses at Dunbar. God forgive that I should cast aspersion on sincere believers, but can they not see my sincerity and their own true interest?

Most of all, I lacked information and instruction. Had I gone too far on my own initiative or failed to strike out far enough? A settled intelligence is what government needs. But such surveillance must be directed and the results gathered in. I had been cast aside and left to languish in uncertainty.

If a man is shipwrecked on a desert island what should he do? Await instructions? Or set his hand industriously to the tasks before him – shelter, food, manufacture of life's necessities and a system of protection and defence. I was now a castaway, left to work out my own salvation.

Sooner walk the estuary shore and seek a message in a bottle than receive London dispatches.

Yet I was not alone. The city might be crowded and beaten by stormy tides of party spirit and dissent, but here I had a refuge. The house by the Netherbow is my bridge, my cabin, nest and eyrie.

Why was this so different? My loyal Evelina at home, bringing up our children. A dutiful wife through all adversities of fortune, yet I cannot call her confidante or friend. Did I ever have a friend, or was I always the solitary traveller? That was my early lesson, to depend on none but myself. Even then, question, examine, never take on trust. The Lord alone shall be our conscience and our Judge.

Until I met Isobel. A woman of the world endowed with charm, sympathy and wit, to whom I could talk as with an equal. An honest soul, whose place was not bestowed by birth or rank but by her own sense and worth. Looking back, I see that her confidence became the consolation of my spirit. I trusted her with all my heart and though we were sorely tried we are still conjoined by mutual esteem and interest.

Moreover, we became united by practical concerns common to us both. We sought a sensible relation between two neighbours uneasily at peace. And we shared the anxiety of a beautiful young woman exposed to risk and temptation in the corrupting hazard of the times. Or so I believed.

Did I deceive myself through fatherly concern? Isobel Rankin heard me out with patient shrewdness. She knew when to listen and allow her confidante to betray himself. Daniel Foe, master of intelligence, was clay in her supple fingers, but she did not betray me. I may have been blind but she watched for me, protecting my footsteps when others failed. I owe more to Isobel than to any other human person. I have no means of adequately repaying her, but her story shall be told and at least I can render her that service.

And dear Catherine. Ruined, exploited, cast aside. A Niobe with falling locks, bare shoulders, bruised arms, beaten breast. I pictured myself administering comfort.

Although I confess my weakness now, I did keep my feelings tightly reined and they did not divert me from my duties. I tried to pray for guidance but even He could not reveal my obscure path. I could only await the outcome of Parliament's debate.

❧❧❧

The session crawled towards its long-postponed conclusion.

The oak roof beams of the Hall seemed to exude moisture. A clammy press of bodies and warm breath jammed every bench and step and passageway. Only those like Isobel Rankin with some direct patronage were guaranteed a place.

Members had gradually exhausted their capacity for further speech. Seven days of argument for and against negotiating Union had ebbed and flowed. Even the eloquence of Andrew Fletcher of Saltoun was exhausted. The time for declaration and decision had arrived.

Queensberry rose to sum up, resplendent, Mrs Rankin noted, in his golden chain of office and a black silk coat adorned with heraldic insignia. He stepped towards the central table.

'My lords and gentlemen, the great issue – the Union of the ancient kingdoms of Scotland and England – has been debated for many days among us. And in every corner of the land. To treat or not to treat with England. But it is we, the Parliament of Scotland who must decide. That is our prerogative and privilege.

'The long-awaited moment has come to vote. Every argument has been rehearsed, for and against, and every loyalty tested. What is best for the future prosperity of this kingdom? For the security of this realm? Think. Reason. Judge carefully so that we can enter negotiations with a firm resolve.

'Generations still unborn stand our accusers in this hour. Did we decide on some narrow interest? Or did we vote for reason, for conscience, for morality, and for that faith we proudly confess as a Protestant nation? Let posterity be my judge. I vote for Union on advantageous terms.'

Queensberry regained his seat to polite applause.

The heat and fire of the debate had been drawn. Isobel saw Glamis ready to reply. Icy and controlled he sat stiffly upright on the front bench. But it was the Duke of Hamilton who rose to his feet and surveyed the Chamber. Scotland's premier aristocrat was kingly in red and gold. A lavish, curling wig framed his angular face. Isobel watched with familiar fascination as Hamilton raised his head in an attempt to project his receding chin, only managing to thrust upward his protuberant nose.

'His lordship has spoken eloquently and briefly.' The words were clear and precise but underlaid by nasal drawl. 'If only the Laird of Saltoun had exercised such restraint.' This drew a smattering of laughter. 'We do not endorse Mr Fletcher's republican utopias so I shall emulate his lordship's good example.

'For those engaged in clamorous debate this moment has crept upon you like a thief in darkness. For others among us the clear light of hereditary principle has shone like a beacon from the first. Let nothing now be done to our dishonour, the dishonour of the Estates of Scotland or of that ancient crown and sceptre that sit as sacred talismans before you. His lordship, the Queen's Commissioner, describes our heavy duty in this matter. I recognise that duty but remember too our rights. No one sits here but holds some part of Scotland at his own disposal. What shall we who hold the hills and valleys, fields and forests, towns and harbours, have from Union? The loss of ancient privilege and independence? The loss of what is ours by blood and charter?

'It is too soon to cast all that into the scales. Stay your hand and vote against negotiation. The patriotic issue is still undecided. Defend your natural interest against unproven benefits and untried risks.'

A rumble of assent was heard. Some feet stamped. Hamilton was done.

'I thank your lordship. Record the vote.'

It was a clever speech, appealing to self-interest without ruling out the possibility of Union in itself. If as seemed likely the vote went against him, Hamilton would still be a powerful influence. Isobel wryly saw in it the love of indecision she had come to know so well. Members leaned forward anxious to be done and escape into the busy warmth of taverns or the refuge of their town houses. The result seemed already as if decided in another court. A future day would bring the battle to appoint Commissioners, and test the strength of every faction in the negotiation.

At the Netherbow normal rules had been suspended. Foe

was in possession of the parlour. Mrs Rankin had got a place in Parliament Hall. She seemed to know so many people in the town but this, as Foe had quickly discovered, was the Edinburgh way. Apart from confidential mail he had quickly abandoned aliases as unsustainable when your different selves might bump into each other twice a day.

Wearily Foe shoved his papers to one side. Technical matters were usually absorbing, but not at this juncture. He felt fobbed off, held at one remove from the real issues, and from the motives of the guiding players. This commission could wait; the professional in Foe never missed a deadline.

As he moved to a more comfortable seat, Lady O'Kelly came into the room. 'Mr Foe, I did not mean to interrupt you. I was going to sit here until Mrs Rankin comes back,' she said apologetically.

'Please don't let me stop you.' Foe half rose and gestured towards the other side of the fire. 'I've struggled with this paper all evening.'

Catherine took the offered seat. 'What is your subject?'

'Glassmaking in Scotland. An important subject in itself but somehow not so pressing when the fate of a nation is being decided.'

'How long do you think it will go on?' She looked strained and pale, even a little dishevelled compared to her normal immaculate appearance.

'They may talk into the night.'

'It's dark already.' Catherine got up and peered through the narrow window pane. The street was busy but quiet. Expectant.

'How is your own business coming on?' Foe directed

a sympathetic glance towards the figure at the window, taking in the elegant shoulders and the gently curved structure of the long back.

Catherine turned round and met his gaze. 'The lawyers are almost done. With this duty and that commission they have the legacy reduced to a manageable size – the price of my passage home.'

'Professional fees are the curse of honest trades.'

'Which professions do you mean?' She folded herself gracefully back into the chair.

'All of them, but especially lawyers. They tie up a straightforward enterprise in knots and when they bring it to its knees they summon you to hearings in chancery, the cost of which exceeds your original loss.'

'You seem to speak from experience.'

'I have endured my own misfortunes.'

'In love or just in trade, Mr Foe?'

Their eyes met again but Foe averted his in the direction of the burning coals. 'I have a dear wife, Lady O'Kelly, and seven children. I have been sorely tried but my greatest sorrow is that they have had to share my tribulation.'

'Your tenderness does you credit.' Catherine leaned back into her chair. 'Mrs Foe does not enjoy travel?'

'She takes good care of our children.'

'Such is the reward of a stable union.'

'Indeed, but you have suffered a terrible loss.' Foe tactfully discarded his own hardships. 'I fear I am not able to convey the comfort that I intend.' He leaned forward. 'You must treat me as a companion and as a means of friendly support.'

Catherine looked again at the neat intense features and the grey eyes, which had a hint of softness in them. 'Poor Mr Foe, I believe that you are gallant at heart.'

As she spoke, Mrs Rankin came hurriedly into the room, shedding cloak and gloves.

'It's over.'

'They've voted!' exclaimed Foe.

'For negotiations. With a comfortable majority. The streets are bizzin like bees in a fyke.' She hurried back towards the window. Foe was up and helping push home the shutters and drop the bars. Catherine did not move.

'Who will negotiate for Scotland?'

Foe and Mrs Rankin turned together. She paced more slowly over to the fire.

'Commissioners appointed by the Queen.'

'By the Queen!' Foe could not repress his surprise and excitement.

'Where was the Jacobite vote?' Catherine was suddenly on her feet.

'After the main vote when the Hall was half-empty and members straggling out, Hamilton moved that the Commissioners to negotiate the treaty be appointed by the Queen.'

'Hamilton!' Catherine exclaimed.

'This means Union. It is as good as sealed if Queen Anne puts in her own men,' Foe cut in.

'The benches were astonished,' agreed Mrs Rankin responding to Foe's mood. 'Half the opposition vote was already in the taverns. They thought that business was finished for the night.'

'Has the Duke surrendered his resistance?'

'Who knows what he intends. But it seems your cause is triumphant. Unless, God forbid, this starts a war.'

Catherine had been silent and immobile beside the fire. She rose to her feet. 'I must go upstairs.' Paler than ever, she left quickly through the door, which had remained open since Mrs Rankin's dramatic entry.

Foe looked towards the older woman, a question forming on his lips. But Mrs Rankin had begun to sway. He rushed forward and helped her into Catherine's fireside chair.

'Please, Mr Foe, a glass. I was all but overrun by the crowd.'

Foe hurried to the brandy decanter and returned with a full tumbler. 'I must go out to witness these scenes.'

'No, you mustn't go out. They are trying to march on Parliament. The government men ran for their carriages. I saw the Lord Chancellor brought to a halt by the mob. Listen.' A dull rumble punctuated with angry yells could be heard beyond the shutters. 'Pray God he had the sense to get out and walk before they broke his coach in pieces. Please, Mr Foe, remain here with me.'

It was as much appeal as warning and Foe could not refuse. He poured himself a glass of claret and took the other fireside seat.

'This is a momentous day, Mrs Rankin. Despite the mob, we must have a toast.'

'Please, no more speeches. I have had my fill of speeches.'

'Yet we should not stint on ceremony. My dear Mrs Rankin, I give you the concord, no, the harmonious union, of our two ancient nations. The Union.'

'The Union, Mr Foe. So long as it does not replace claret with English ale.'

'No, my lesson has been learned. That is to put English prayer books in Scottish kirks. I would not trespass on Scots liberties even if I could. No, it is the government and commerce of this nation that need improvement.'

'Will the English improve Scotland?' Mrs Rankin's

brandy appeared to be having a restorative effect.

'This is a gallant and religious people. The country is good and the soil in many places capable of improvement. All that is wanting is English Art and English Trade.'

'You sound like a periodical. What about English interference? You destroyed our colony at Darien, Mr Foe, by blockading trade.'

'I see that you are no stranger to business. There is some truth in what you say, for the London merchants would brook no competition. But that is precisely why this Union will be the saving of Scottish trade.'

'Then we shall be British and prosper together.' The brandy being finished, Foe fetched two more clarets. 'You are a man of the future, Mr Foe,' Mrs Rankin observed.

'Trade is a secret wisdom that unlocks our future. I give you a toast. Future prospects!'

'Future prospects.'

The yells and cries outside seemed to be coming closer. They both drew nearer to the fire. Mrs Rankin threw on more coals.

'I am sorry that Lady O'Kelly did not stay to help us celebrate. She seemed anxious,' said Foe.

'She has had a trying time.'

Staring towards the reviving blaze, Foe missed a sharp look which shot across the hearth. 'So I understand. She was telling me just before you came back that lawyers have frittered away her legacy with charges and procedures.'

'Perhaps Lady O'Kelly was a little hasty in coming to Edinburgh.'

'In what way?' Foe's well-trained ear detected a confiding tone.

'Her affairs were uncertain, and she has used her time here to renew old acquaintances. I believe that Lady

Catherine first met her husband in Edinburgh, and that they belonged to a dissolute circle.'

'I noticed she looked strained, like some one lacking sleep.'

'Not everyone in Edinburgh observes the Presbyterian virtues. I think I warned you of that circumstance, Mr Foe.'

'You suspect impropriety?' For a moment his mask of assured control had slipped.

'Perhaps I am over-anxious.' Having stirred the pot, Mrs Rankin left it to simmer. 'There are so many temptations in the path of an attractive widow.'

'You are a woman of sense,' Foe responded, 'like so many of your underrated sex. Your prudence does you credit.'

'Are you a revolutionary, Mr Foe?'

'With equal education women would be managers as much as men. Growing up without birth or connections, I see the world differently from those who have both.'

Mrs Rankin studied the attentive face opposite for any sign of insincerity and found none. 'It is not easy to advance by your own efforts,' she admitted.

'And fortune can be capricious – or a whore. Religion is our consolation. The hand of the Lord is not withdrawn even in our darkest hour.'

She realised that Foe was addressing his own need for conviction; there was no trace of irony. 'What if God is cut off from us by our sins?' His honesty had provoked her.

'Then we confess to Him and He is ready to forgive.'

'Of course.' She could go no further down that path.

'However, I think you are mistaken about Lady O'Kelly,' Foe resumed. 'She could not be involved in any dishonourable trade.'

'What can a defenceless woman barter except her honour?'

'Shame on any man who would make that purchase.'

'What if the woman strikes the bargain for herself?' Mrs Rankin pressed.

'What could be equivalent to a woman's virtue?'

At that moment, Catherine appeared cloaked and already pulling up her hood.

'Excuse my rudeness. I must find a ship immediately.'

'You cannot risk the mob,' Foe said sharply.

'The gates will be closed early. No-one will leave Edinburgh tonight,' Mrs Rankin's voice betrayed a quiver of alarm.

'I am packed ready for the White Horse stage. Goodbye, Mr Foe, I hope that we will meet again.'

'Are you sure this is wise? The mood of the town is ugly. Let me take your trunk and...'

'I'll get a cadie for the trunk,' Mrs Rankin intervened. Catherine started towards the landing. 'We can go through the back court. Please, Mr Foe, stay here, I know my way.'

Mrs Rankin followed the younger woman out. Foe looked after them, surprised and curious.

Within the hour Mrs Rankin returned without further comment and retired to bed. As soon as she was settled Foe slipped down the turnpike. Staying in the shadow of the lower landing, he looked out over the street.

The angry rumble had become a roar of voices. Men, women and children were hurling stones, timber from stalls and stinking rubbish at a retreating line of the city guard, who had formed a barrier of pikes in a doomed attempt to ward off the hail of missiles. They were being forced back towards the Netherbow Port where a few of their number were desperately trying to push the gates shut against another crowd advancing up the Canongate. The whole scene of riot was luridly lit with blazing torches.

The High Street column crept forward like a menacing crouching beast, headed by two drummers and rhythmically measured by thundering cries of 'No Union! No Union! No Union!' Foe's practised eye scanned round looking for the agitators and ringleaders, but the mass seemed to be moving by instinct rather than by design. An implacable force of nature.

The guards' line began to break and pikes and halberds were torn from their grasp. Some fled into the closes. Others were caught and pulled down beneath the mob. Amidst a striking, beating turmoil their uniforms were torn off and tossed into the air.

Like a crashing wave before which the breakwater had succumbed, the crowd swirled into the arches of the Port. The remaining guards disappeared from view and the heavy studded gates were forced back. The two columns met beneath the central archway, merged and mingled. Then, as if picking up another scent, the whole mass reformed and started down the Canongate.

Foe watched as more and more people followed, now an ordered stream, purposeful and resolute, torches held high. They were tradesmen, prentices and serving-women, with here and there a well-cut jacket or tailored coat. Yet all were submerged in one identity of protest. Swords, clubs and staves were brandished.

'No Union! No Union! No Union!'

Foe wondered how many mansions would be besieged that night. Every Scottish noble seemed to maintain his own armed troop and deaths seemed likely. As the marching column began to thin into onlookers and beggars, Foe retreated up the turnpike, pushing the landing door firmly shut. Soon he was ensconced, high above the storm-tossed streets. Whatever the hubbub of the mob, his arguments had won the day, he thought with a sense of inner exultation. There would be negotiation. Reasoned compromise would prevail.

PART TWO

I WAS BORN in the village of Dunkeld which lies between

Perth and Blair Castle, hereditary seat of the Murrays, the Dukes of Atholl. My mother was the daughter of a poor Episcopalian minister. At my birth her parents cut her off, and she moved from a comfortable stone built house at Moulinearn to a Highland hovel by the River Tay.

My father, I was later told, had been a nephew of the Duke himself, a younger son who interspersed his military service with hunting, drinking and whoring on the family estates. I believe that he sent some money to my mother, and although he died abroad a few years after my birth I was always allowed to bear the proud name of Murray: Aeneas Murray.

As a youngster I knew nothing of my origins and cared less. Our cluster of turf and mud cottages was alive with children of every age, and with animal life. From dawn to dark we ran free amidst the dogs, goats and poultry. And when we ventured out beyond the messy hive, a world of beauty and adventure beckoned.

On every side, woods climbed steeply from the village. The slopes were alive with birch, oak, ash and hazel, and offered endless battlefields, canopies and burrows. As they thinned, pine trees pointed on towards high hilltops and rocky cliffs. Through everything the river ran, an unceasing silver stream that patterned all our seasons, sometimes with flood and spate, sometimes with gentle golden currents. It seemed the source of everything that upheld life. Fresh water, fish of speckled silver brown and gold, and the cleansing flow that carried off the dirt and muck.

But most of all, the river was a play of light. In every mood and season it embodied changes of colour and of variant motion. These were our daily occupation and delight, and to this day if I close my eyes I can hear the river purl and dip my hand or foot in its cold ripples.

Yet I can barely remember a single name from that time, just a maze of faces. They were all Gaelic names of course – Mhairis, Domhnalls, Ruaraidhs. What happened to that passionate band of outlaws? No doubt some were in the army at the Battle of Sherriffmuir years later, unremembered and unrecognised by me. Of my Gaelic little more than a smattering of words and phrases remains. It has had no part in my life since that reverse, but it was my mother's tongue, and in Dunkeld it named everything around me.

On Sundays, though, I was taken to the kirk. On every side were scattered ruins of a noble cathedral but one part was roofed and enclosed. We sat on hard wooden pews and heard the service read in English or more likely Scots. We used an Episcopal prayer book much resented by the Presbyterian zealots and yet delivered in the harsh tones of narrow Protestantism. Sermons were to be endured. Colour, pattern, and rhythm were absent. This was the public world to which we must conform. On other days I could run free through the green meadow between the river and the ruins. On Sundays my mother held me firmly by the hand and walked me from the village to the kirk.

If stern Bible readings failed to feed my imagination, it was nourished by village tales of ghosts, warrior clans, lost loves, old priests and monks, and of the great Colmcille. When the Vikings burnt Iona Abbey, his sacred relics were brought to Dunkeld. I do not recall who taught me these things; they were rarely mentioned in the everyday world of our home at least. But they were in the landscape and the consciousness of the people. Occasionally a harper or a seanachaidh would arrive and we youngsters would squeeze into the chosen cottage, amidst the reek of peat, clay pipes and damp, steaming clothes. No more regarded than the dogs stretched beside us on the mud floor, we heard eulogies, laments for long-lost chiefs, tales of Finn Ossian and the Fian, and traditions of Columba Dove of the Church. It is hard now to distinguish what I heard then from what I learnt later. I remember one song of soul sadness at leaving Ireland which I never heard since. Why is it that things of fifty years ago remain fresh and clear, while events of adulthood fade into indistinguishable greyness?

There was a school at Dunkeld tied to the kirk. The older children had tales of beatings and of the hard strangeness of the teacher's tongue. Like the black-coated minister, he belonged to a different world. The village deferred but went its own way in its own language. My life was in the woods and on the river banks and I found true echoes of that life in the music and the poetry of the ceilidh house.

Then suddenly everything changed. I was seven years old when a letter came to my mother. A few days later we were on the road to Perth and I was sent to school. Was the message that my father had died, leaving provision in his will for my education? Or was it because King William came to the throne of the Stewarts that year? James went into exile, Presbyterians gained the upper hand, and every landed house made its dispositions for changed circumstances. So perhaps I was to be prepared for a new kind of usefulness. Having long since lost my Murray connection, I cannot now tell. Strange as it may seem, of Bonnie Dundee and the battle at Killiecrankie I recall nothing. We had already left Dunkeld.

The cobbled vennels of Perth were choked with brown and green filth. Animals were butchered in the market place, their blood running into open sewers. Everything was trade, noise and bustle, a cacophony of raucous chapmen, street criers and beggars. That was how the Fair City sounded to a frightened country boy.

We lived in a close off South Street and every day I had to walk to school, where I was taught by Mr Gilfillan, a kindly dominie, though strict when application slackened. But he saw my dilemma and allowed me to catch up at my own pace. The other boys taunted my broken English and thick Highland accent. Each day I ran the gauntlet of class bullies until, after a time, I became familiar and accepted.

I explored the town street by street. My habit was to wander after school but whatever the sights I would soon be drawn to the river. This mighty sullen flow was my sweet Tay, swollen and sometimes fierce with threatening flood. The quay was often full with masted ships disgorging or loading cargoes of timber, salted herring and hides for curing. I looked longingly across the bridge at the slopes and woods of Kinnoull, but for now I was forbidden the other bank. Like a lonely scout I was left gazing downriver to remote untravelled countries.

There was little enough these days to attract me home. My mother had no company in Perth and kept poor health. Our relationship had always been something I took for granted but it seemed to lack any depths or strength to develop in our changed circumstances. More times than not I would find her drowsing at the fire, a glass and empty bottle tumbled by her chair. I fended for myself, raking in the press for bread or an end of cheese. I stirred the ashes to keep us warm until, driven by the cold, she would stumble over to the recessed bed. Then I would lay out my rug on the floor.

We were not entirely friendless. Mr Gilfillan took interest

in my progress. My ready mind eagerly embraced English as a second language, and Latin as a third. I responded to his encouragement with enthusiasm, having perhaps no other source of warmth. Through his recommendation, a well-dressed older lady came to our one-roomed house and spoke with my mother. From then on, between the visits of this aristocratic person, little gifts of food and money arrived regularly at our door. She was an austere figure, tall and silver-haired, with high cheekbones, and dressed always in black lace and velvet. Her name was Lady Glamis.

In the two years or more that we had lived in Perth, my mother and I had not attended the kirk. Now, at our benefactor's prompting, she began to go to a private chapel in a great house near the Inch. I was left at home poring over a book, since these too had begun to appear in our house.

So it was that when later that year she fell into a new weakness, I sat by the fire and read to her from the stories of Aesop, or from Julius Caesar's account of his campaigns in Gaul. A serving woman came from Lady Glamis to cook and wash. She must also have been the source of the sherry and Madeira wine, which my poor mother now quaffed on a daily basis. It seemed to ease her pain. A doctor also attended, but without lasting effect. Within a few months of her relapse, my mother died. Messages were sent but no-one appeared from Moulinearn or Dunkeld. She was buried in Blackfriars graveyard, in the course of a cruel frost that caused the men to light a fire so that they could break open the ground and lower her coffin.

It seems a hard admission: I felt little sense of grief or loss. Looking back I see the sadness of her life but since I had outgrown her skirts we had not been close. I lived with her rather than for her and struck out to make an existence for myself. She had no means to break out or to find her way back to first foundations. I remember her now with gratitude, exercising a consolation of my creed by praying for the progress of her soul.

Nor at the time was I anxious or afraid. It seemed throughout as if everything had been arranged. I went to lodge with Mr Gilfillan's aunt, a kindly matron whose own children had grown up and left the nest. She fed and cosseted me then left me to my own devices. Each week without fail I went to the great house by the Inch to eat dinner with Lady Glamis and give her news of my studies.

I began now to live for books. The town and its environs were a habitual backdrop, but each new printed volume brought its own voyage of discovery. From Caesar's Gallic Wars I went to Virgil and my heroic namesake, pious Aeneas the faithful wanderer. I was deep in Greek as well and veered between plotting the adventures of Odysseus in the original and racing through his voyages in an English translation. I was given Shakespeare and Chaucer along with the Scots makars and Hector Boece's history of the Scottish nation. An invisible hand fed my imagination, while the town and its environs receded into the background.

On Sundays I attended Lady Glamis' chapel on condition that I kept what happened there to myself. To whom would my revelations have been addressed? Yet even as a boy I knew that this was not religion as the Protestants understood it, whether Presbyterian or Episcopalian in Scotland. The brocaded altar was surmounted by a crucifix in black and gold. Christ's body gleamed by candlelight, and when the priest raised his cup he seemed to offer a drink to the suffering Saviour. Incense filled the room, which was situated in the very top of the house beneath the rafters. The solemn language of the mass embraced the form and pattern of my Latin poets and the drama of my Greek tragedians. I do not think my sleeping soul was yet roused but some seed of intuition was sown deep in my impressionable spirit.

Who was the priest? I did not know, nor ever thought to ask. Does that seem extraordinary, given what I was to become? Then I was more conscious of myself, the sounds and sensations, and of Lady Glamis, stately and severe yet always attentive to my emotions and concerns. I realised that this was Catholic, Papist in the parlance of the street, but I did not understand the pressures which faithful Romans endured. Or the dangers of search, trial and execution that a missionary priest in Scotland ran. Later I drained that cup to its dregs.

I must have been eleven or twelve, firmly established at the grammar school in Perth, when I was first taken to the castle. By then, though still lodged in the High Street with Aunt Gilfillan, I spent most evenings at the Inch, where I kept my books and was allowed the freedom of a little panelled room lit with candles and warmed by its own fire, summer and winter. Occasionally I went to the houses of other boys from school. Mainly I lived in my private world, touched only by Lady Glamis and her kindly servants, who fed and clothed me. Mine was a cocooned existence, without past or future. I had no idea how, with that journey, everything would start to change.

It was a bright sharp morning as the coach climbed out of Perth and over the hill. Behind us, the Tay flowed on towards its distant silvery firth. Trees came stepping down the wooded slopes to gather round the road as the now reviving horses cantered through a breezy sunshine. The Sidlaw Hills were to our right, while to the north the misty blues of Cairngorm seemed suspended in the sky. Not to see, not to feel the pulse of my own country has been the hardest aspect of my adult path.

We clattered on through farm towns and hamlets until we reached the douce high street of Coupar Angus. Cultivated rigs, sheep and cattle in every pen and fold, the stone cottage and green kail patch: everything was new to me. In the late afternoon we turned into a pillared gateway ornamented with two roaring lions. Before us rose the mighty sandstone tower of Glamis, Scotland's royal standard fluttering in the ramparts.

A tall nobleman waiting for us at the inner gate stepped forward to hand Lady Glamis from the coach. I barely noticed him, my eyes being fixed on the burly men in bonnets and leather jerkins who were ranged around the courtyard tending their horses and their weapons.

'You look well, mother,' the nobleman said to Lady Glamis.

'Well enough. Why do you have the tenants at arms?' she replied.

I recall very little of what then transpired. We were taken into a long, vaulted chamber and food and drinks were brought. I was sent willingly to explore while my Lord and Lady talked. Overawed by the scale of this ancient fortress and palace, I did not stray far. Later I was to know Glamis well. Soon I was beckoned to an upper chamber and introduced to a grey-haired man in a black cassock. We sat at a deeply polished table on which books lay open or in piles, leather-bound with gold-tooled spines. He asked me gently about my studies and my reading. Comforted by the sight of books, I warmed to his interest and showed off my juvenile knowledge. He coaxed me further, asking about my attendance at the private chapel. I responded by reciting long sections of the mass by heart.

'Well done, Aeneas, good boy,' he said laying a hand on my black, unruly curls. 'I think that you are definitely ready.'

The last thing I remember is falling asleep before a huge fire beneath the elaborate plasterwork of a lofty drawing room. The day's events had overtaken me. Within a week I was leaving Scotland on ship for Flanders and the Catholic seminary at Louvain.

Dear Mr Foe,

I am sending on your papers and mail as you requested. To be honest I was astonished when you explained how your news pages written in Edinburgh appeared in London. Now I have seen these sheets for myself. I hope you will find these ones satisfactory. I cannot pretend to any knowledge of such political controversy. Is this a new form of trade – in words? Are you still a man of business, even in your letters? Forgive me for teasing – you will agree, this puts you in a new light after the last few months of our acquaintance. I know you explained it all to me but sometimes you talk very quickly and it is only later that I think to ask. I do feel that you are trying to present Scotland in a good light, for it seems not everyone in London loves the Scots.

No news of our recent guest. We must hope that she reached Ireland safely and that her affairs are not so bad as she feared. Edinburgh continues agitated about the negotiations. Every evening is uneasy. But the main men are all in London so overall things are quieter. The Duke of Hamilton remains at his estate and takes no part, which makes everyone wonder. What will the opposition do now? I confess that my own feelings are still divided, yet I can see the force of your persuasions.

I hope that your travels are going well. Insist on seeing your room, and especially the bed, before engaging. The Saracen's Head is trustworthy but depend on nothing north of the Forth without inspection. I look forward to receiving the travel sheets as arranged. I find your impressions of Scotland interesting and entertaining. Of course they are most instructive too.

      With sincere compliments,

                    Mrs Isobel Rankin

My dear Mrs Rankin,

I am very obliged for your kindness in sending on my papers. They were waiting for me safely at the Saracen's Head in Glasgow. My journey through the southwest has been most instructive, but I was sick of Galloway through which the travelling is very rough – the roads as well as the entertainment. However, I was well received by the gentlemen of these parts. They are very courteous. I shall send you some account of them in my next papers.

Like all writers I must draw on my existing stock to feed an avaricious public. This is indeed a business in which the trick is to ensure that demand exceeds supply – at some personal cost to the poor workhorse of supply. The sheets that I am returning for delivery to the White Horse are my description of Edinburgh. I hope that you will be pleased with my impressions of your native town. I am anxious you may be offended by my strictures on the magistrates for not draining the loch and extending northwards.

I am relieved to hear of the gradual end to tumult and riot in your narrow wynds and streets, not least as it touches on your own safety. A more expansive town would allow the mob to be more easily controlled and quelled. At times during the late disturbance it felt like a revolution in the state. Lady O'Kelly is safer out of Edinburgh. I am sure that in due course we will have better news. When everything in London has been settled a new age of peace and prosperity will begin.

The weather is fine here and I hope you enjoy the same. Please accept my warmest thanks and cordial greeting,

Yours respectfully,

Daniel Foe.

My dear Nellie,

Have you heard anything of Catherine? Please keep a sharp eye out for her – her departure was so sudden as to be suspicious. You are the only person she knows to go to out of Edinburgh, as far as I am aware, though of course now she is mixed up with who knows what kind of people. These are confusing times. Boats from Leith to Ireland are not so frequent and a coach to Glasgow seems more likely.

Why did she not come to me at the moment of crisis? Was it always that way, Nellie? – Did she always make her own decisions. Even when she was young and we were so close, did she really confide in me or was there a stranger behind that lovely face? Does Catherine have anyone in the wide world whom she can wholly trust? Enough, these regrets and memories only make me melancholy.

I am young no longer.

Things are much quieter here since Mr Foe has gone off on his travels. He aims to describe Scotland for the English in the hope that familiarity may breed affection. I told you Mr Foe believes in progress as in religion. We could describe for him poor souls starving in the roadside sheughs for want of grain in those Darien years. Or Highland women lying bloody in the snow after the Glencoe atrocity. But Daniel Foe will not pen such pictures, for he has the art of telling people what they want to hear. Subtly though as a man of letters, his new profession. I could describe him for you, Nellie, very neat and precise with quick well-formed features moving above a comfortable chin and neck. He stands only inches taller than me and in truth we are both amiably rounded. I confess I am missing Mr Foe, but not in the way you think. He is good company if you can keep up with his talking.

Edinburgh is calmer now even at night. The lairds have gone back to their estates. Why not come and keep me company? Could Glasgow not do without you for a while? I might almost be taking to loneliness were it not for a particular message. Yes, I have been keeping that one quiet. The Duke is at Kinneil. The rage of combat has subsided and his faithful consort remains at her English house nursing her brood like the sow her farrow. So the old boar turns a bit itchy and restless. Or has some other purpose.

Nellie, I cannot write more about this. Please come to Edinburgh and advise me. Then if need be you could keep house here. Truly it could be unwise, even risky, given his part in these public affairs. I will not go to Holyrood. At least, dear Nellie, I have someone I can trust. Please do not delay replying – the post is quite reliable.

    I look to see you soon,
        Your own,
            Isobel

After two years at the seminary I was allowed to return to

Glamis for the summer, and that became the pattern. As my long education drew to a close it seemed natural if not inevitable that I should be assigned to Scotland and serve the network of great houses and private chapels that kept Catholicism alive. At the centre of that web was Glamis and this was the connection that brought me to Edinburgh and to the defining crisis of my existence. Which also broke the connection.

I came back a changed person from that first summer visit. Louvain roused me into human society and ended my long sleep of isolation, my retreat before the blows of fortune.

The seminary was a company of boys growing fast into young men, a place of friendship, boisterous games and earnest study. Only some were like me intended for the priesthood – Catholic families often sent their sons to seminary school to ensure a gentlemanly education in the faith. We rode, fenced and shot, as well as translated and debated. At seminary I stumbled on my talent for drawing and painting, which the priests actively encouraged. Religion was the sustaining foundation of our days but it did not constrain our growth or suppress our spirits.

Scots were in the majority, both among the staff and pupils. My particular friends included John Maxwell from Dumfriesshire, William Menzies of Pitfoddels in Aberdeenshire, and Hector MacDonald of Kinlochmoidart. They were the best of company in good times and in bad.

From the staff, Father MacIntyre was a fine teacher of the Classics, among which I continued to thrive. He also gave French and Italian classes, both of which I attended. Father Maxwell, Principal of the seminary and John's uncle, taught philosophy and theology, which I respected without particular enthusiasm. It was Father Innes who gained my special devotion.

His history classes were focused on the ongoing mission and development of the Church, but he made a special study of the history of Scotland in relation to his theme. First came the aeons of geological time, the ice ages, and the early settlement of the land by hunter gatherers. He pictured the landscape taking its familiar shape with mountain, river wood and corrie inhabited by bear, elk, beaver, deer and wolves.

Then he conjured the invading tribes – Picts, Celts, Brythons, Scots, Romans, Saxons. Here was the clash of peoples, cultures and beliefs, until with new light from the east came Ninian, Columba and the rest. The idea of Scotland as a Christian nation had begun and when with the onslaught of the Vikings the relics of Columba were moved to Dunkeld, a union of Pict and Scot was consummated on the altar.

This was the great motif of Father Innes' lectures, how the Church had encouraged and sustained a Scottish nation. Through the long wars of independence against England, when Scotland had been brought time and again to forced submission, her hard-won status as a daughter of the Holy See preserved our right to nationhood. In that dusty classroom, we stood in Rome with Baldred Bissett to plead our cause, detailing the ancient origins of Scotland, the Stone of Scone on which our kings were crowned, the special protection of St Andrew guaranteed by the translation of the Holy Apostle's relics to our shores, and the Holy Father's gifts to Scotland's kings of the sword and sceptre. We learned the Declaration of Arbroath by heart. I was left in little doubt that our purpose in life was to restore that nationhood to Scotland and with it the true freedom and dignity of faith.

Innes was historian, missionary and storyteller all in one. His classes changed my way of seeing because they broke down the barriers between my own experience and book learning. The Romans had been at Dunkeld, and I had played around the Pictish fort on Dunsinane Hill. Without realising it, I had sat in dull pews within the very walls that had housed Colmcille's sacred relics. I myself was part of that long story of Scottish freedom and struggle. Emotion and intellect came together in this cause, which was more real and immediate than theological abstractions of Church doctrine or Aristotelian philosophy. Scotland became my high and holy passion, filling the gap left by my early losses.

My friendships at seminary were close but drew short of erotic love. The older students learned about sex through a local madam who looked indulgently on priests in training, and shrewdly gauged the market of untried desires. The college authorities seemed to look elsewhere. But my love for Scotland remained inviolate.

Coming back to Glamis I was treated more like a young relation than a dependant. Lady Glamis was visibly failing but age seemed to unbend her. She listened with fond indulgence to my stories of life in Louvain. In return, she evoked her girlhood and youth amidst Scotland's wars of religion. She recalled her encounters with the Marquis of Montrose, leader of the royalist cause, and her friendships with the extended Graham kin. The final doom of Montrose and the wasting of spiritual vision after King Charles' restoration had led to her conversion. For her, religious faith shone like a beacon through the greed for power and wealth that dominated aristocratic life in Scotland.

Lord Glamis took no part in these conversations. He

rode out to show me his wide fertile acres beneath the Cairngorms. We also went hunting in the beautiful Angus glens – Prosen, Clova and Glen Isla. On our journeys in search of game, we visited remote farms and cottages where the appearance of my Lord of Glamis commanded instant respect and obedience. Many of the armed retainers at his lordship's call were men of the glens. He was a fine horseman and always ready to improve my skills and knowledge. He displayed no interest in the seminary or my education there, treating me like a young cousin, with offhand kindness.

Often Glamis seemed distant and preoccupied with political business. Messengers arrived from all parts and sometimes he hurried off to Edinburgh, staying a week or more in pursuit of some conference or connection. I did not realise it then, but he was deeply implicated in the Darien expedition to Panama and in its disastrous consequences for the personal and public finances of the Scots. In winter time Glamis would sometimes travel to Court in London but during these months I was in Louvain and he never spoke to me about the royal succession as one by one the Stewarts died childless. All, that is, except our rightful king.

Later our relationship was to change in every way. When I returned to Scotland as a priest, I was based at Glamis but journeying across the north, Tayside and into Fife. By then old Lady Glamis had died, remembering me kindly in her will, and a new young wife had come to take her title and her share in my Lord's affections. I became their confessor and sensed more acutely his distance and remoteness.

The older Lady's ability to create a social atmosphere at Glamis was sadly missed. My own role as a dependant was now more clearly defined and it ruled out casual banter across the dinner table. I did not feel it was my place to advise or intervene as Lady Glamis became depressed and discontented. She consoled herself with frequent visits to relations and long stays in Edinburgh. Glamis continued impervious. I was not sorry when my own duties took me away from that uncomfortable household and even, for a while, from Scotland.

I had kept in regular contact with Louvain, attending retreats and receiving instructions and counsel from my old teachers. It was on one such visit that Father Maxwell called me to his study and told me that I was summoned to the Court of James III and VII at St Germain. There, I should await further directions concerning my work in Scotland.

I was curious as to the significance of this new development and its bearing on my role and duties, but Maxwell was either unwilling or unable to enlighten me. You must understand, he simply said, that affairs in Britain are coming to a crisis. I knew of course that he meant the succession to Queen Anne, for when that barren branch of the old Stewart tree finally fell, the choice would be between restoring King James to his rightful throne or bringing in German George, a grandson of Elizabeth of Bohemia. The Elector of Hanover offered a Protestant alternative to the legitimate succession. But how was I, a humble missionary priest, concerned with these affairs of state? I felt a new depth in Father Maxwell's benediction. He embraced me warmly and sent me to the bursar for money and clothing suitable for a priest attending Court.

There was little grandeur at St Germain. The chateau was fine enough but full to overcrowding. Every outhouse and stable had been pressed into use for adherents from

Ireland, England, France and Scotland. To eat, you required your own resources or influential patrons at the highest level. Even the meanest day at Glamis exceeded the most lavish standards of King James' pious but penniless regime.

As a priest I was looked after by the religious establishment of the Court. They kept a nearby house packed to the brim with *abbés*, *curés* and *monsignors*, who flitted between Paris, Rome and St Germain, planning a wholly Catholic Europe. From the moment of my arrival, I felt an outsider to this web of intrigue and self-promotion. I ranked low in terms of influence or connection. It appeared that my business lay elsewhere yet no signal or instruction came my way. All the talk was of factions, plots, risings and the timing of a British restoration.

Attending daily audiences in the chateau, hovering at the fringes of the crowd, or walking in the garden, I caught glimpses of the king in exile. He seemed slight, finely formed, melancholy, withdrawn, and intensely pious. Was this the man to inspire rebellion and revolt? The clergy hovered round King James like bees buzzing on a pot of honey.

As the weeks passed in frustrating inaction, I became aware of other more dissolute aspects of Court life. Like the king we were protected and screened from the daily scrabble for existence, but reception rooms which hosted decorous audiences by day were the scene of dancing, drinking and gambling by night. Underlying all this hectic fever of activity was less a chronic insecurity about Britain's political fate than an immediate lack of coin.

The Jacobite Court in exile was no great institute of state, yet it was a hive of contradictions. People lived in their own mutually exclusive orbits of influence and lifestyle. There seemed to be no central guidance or direction, something for which the Vatican, for all it failings, cannot be arraigned. I had come in search of purpose but had found none. Until my first meeting with Catherine.

The day began as normal, with early prayers and mass. After breakfast I received a message to attend on the Earl of Perth, the king's principal Secretary. I hurried across to the chateau immediately but was kept waiting in an anteroom for nearly two hours. The wait, though, proved worthwhile, for when I was finally received the Earl himself laid out the situation plainly.

Queen Anne might pass away at any moment, but the Scottish Parliament had not confirmed a Protestant succession for German Geordie. The English government, if not its people, was pressing hard for an incorporating Union with the northern kingdom that would close forever the back door to its own security and territory. This much I already knew in outline. What I did not know was that a Jacobite rising was imminent in Scotland, harnessing national sentiment against Union. An emissary had already gone from St Germain to treat with influential sympathisers in both Scotland and England, and assure them of military support from France.

However, many of the most powerful nobles were closely watched, and often in the public eye, especially in Scotland. Counted in the opposition ranks were some of the greatest in the land. It had therefore been decided to send secret dispatches with more confidential couriers. This was where my usefulness began.

My longstanding connection with Glamis had not been forgotten. Once ardent in the Jacobite and Catholic cause, Lord Glamis was perceived to have undergone a cooling of his patriotic enthusiasm. Or so I was informed, presumably on reliable testimony. The Court was concerned to place a loyal intermediary to this key sympathiser in order to ensure good communications at the decisive moment. Others were also being sent to target important waverers. These go-betweens included a Lady O'Kelly of Balnacross, who had old Edinburgh connections, though she was now a lady-in-waiting to the Queen Mother at St Germain.

We met that same evening. Lady O'Kelly wore a formal Court dress that opened her upper body to startling view. She held her head high, poised on the slender pillar of her white neck; all was in turn crowned by a plume of glossy black hair. I was a priest but I saw her with my painter's eye. She was like a being from another realm.

I was clumsy and tongue-tied but she was kindly and informative about Edinburgh. I nodded and listened and mimed appreciative agreement. Then we shook hands.and I left the chateau still for the time being Father Aeneas Murray. But her image had entered my soul. My course had leapt from one stream to another, without preparation or decision, yet with a vital impulse that could not be denied.

෪෪෪

Dear Mr Foe,

I have read your observations on Edinburgh with great pleasure. How well you describe the situation and prospects of our city. A loyal citizen, and if truth be told in Edinburgh that could well mean an irate defender of privileges and tradition, might take offence from the conclusions which you base on our confined crowding on a narrow rock. As if the people were not willing to live as sweet and clean as other nations, but delighted in stench and nastiness. Were you too slow to dodge the deluge when gardyloo was called in the narrow wynds and closes?

You do however make amends, and I am quick to acknowledge your fairness in these lines which I have copied out for future use. 'The main street is the most spacious, the longest and best inhabited street in Europe. Its length I have described; the buildings are surprising both for strength, for beauty and for height.' Were we to describe Edinburgh for travellers and for visitors we could not do better. Sometimes I think that our city's future may lie in the admiration and interest of those from other nations. I hope that you have found Glasgow equally pleasing and look forward to your new sheets.

I was though very surprised to find no mention in your account of the ladies of Edinburgh, sometimes acclaimed as the flooers of Auld Reikie. Do they not rank among your estimate of our attractions? It seems not. Your self-denial also extends to scenes of entertainment though admittedly these are hard to find outwith the taverns. We have no theatre since royalty abandoned us. Our kirks are of course plentiful. And Scots are praised by you as reverential almost to a fault. Did you have some special purpose in this portrait, which I myself find hard to recognise?

There I have gone too far. Please forgive this too formal letter in response to your official musings. You must indulge a woman's sharp eye and observations, my dear Mr Foe. This is most unlike my social self and due entirely to your official dispatches from our country. What could be more provoking or more telling than an Englishman's account of Scotland?

I trust you found the Saracen's Head to your satisfaction. I am only sorry that my good friend Mrs MacConnachie was unable to call on you there. As it turned out she came on a short visit to Edinburgh, staying with me in your old lodgings by the Netherbow. I have of course kept your own room reserved and look forward to when you yourself will return to your familiar haunts in our capital city.

With warmest good wishes for your travels,

Yours kindly,

Isobel Rankin

My dear Mrs Rankin,

I have your last letter safely to hand here in Dundee. Thank you for your kind attention to me and to my poor efforts to represent your native land now emerging from the long sleep of sloth and inaction.

Glasgow is indeed a very fine city, perhaps the cleanest, most beautiful and best built in Britain, London excepted. I was most impressed by the university, the finest of any I have seen in Scotland – very high and august in its architecture and situation by the ancient cathedral. The square towers and handsome spire of that edifice truly speak of an age in which devotion and learning were the highest ornament.

But Glasgow is above all a city of commerce. Here is the busy face of trade, foreign as well as domestic, The city is set fair to improve in both. The Union will open doors for the Scots in the American colonies, and though the rabble of Glasgow is making the most determined attempt to prevent Union, its merchants will seize the opportunities offered, for they have the greatest additions to their trade imaginable. Already it appears they are addicted to the illicit bringing in of goods from Virginia, New England and the other colonies. Let those who cannot or would not reap advantage had they the opportunity cast the first stone. For my part I accuse none.

I was hospitably entertained at the Saracen's Head. There I met by chance Colonel Kennedy of Ballintrae, my fencing master. Like me he has been travelling in the southwest and is full of news from these parts. Mainly, I fear, of discontent and agitation against Union.

I went from Glasgow to the Palace of Hamilton, or as we should call it in England Hamilton House. Of course it is by the town of Hamilton, the family being in your turn of speech Hamilton of that ilk. The place may be familiar to you. The house is indeed grand though part of the design is still unfinished. There is a most imposing front with two wings and two more to build when the Duke or his successor pleases. It is a fitting dwelling place for the first of Scotland's noblemen.

I came to Dundee from Perth, a prosperous place with considerable trade to the Baltic, Norway and Russia. The River Tay is navigable to the town for good-sized ships. Their chief export though, is linen, most of which is shipped to England. The salmon taken here and all up and down the river is finely flavoured and prodigious in quantity. They carry it to Edinburgh and barrel it for further transport.

Leaving Perth, I had a desire to see the venerable seat of ceremony for Scottish kings at Scone. Edward I of England, vulgarly supposed a Hammer of the Scots, brought away the old stone on which the monarchs had sat, yet in truth Scotland's kings are still crowned upon it at Westminster. I was told at Scone by a garrulous old man that there is an old Scots prophecy once cut into the stone and now encased within its wooden frame beneath the English throne, that says: 'Or Fates deceived, and Heaven decrees in vain, Or where the stone is found the Scots shall reign.'

But enough of such fables, since even in our own times these old sayings may be abused. It is, however, no fable that at Scone all kings of Scotland were crowned, and that all the rulers of Great Britain have since been crowned above its ancient stone.

From Scone to Dunkeld is so short a way that I went to see where the first skirmish was played out between the forces of King William and the Laird of Claverhouse, later known as Bonnie Dundee. If Dundee had not been killed by an accidental shot, he would certainly have advanced southwards and given Dutch William a journey into the north instead of a voyage to Ireland. But Providence had better things in store for Great Britain and effected a Glorious Revolution in our affairs. You know my sentiments on that matter.

The Firth of Tay also marked the furthest extent of the Roman Empire in Britain. Julius Agricola, the best of generals, pierced further and traversed by land into the heart of the northern Highlands. Yet seeing no end to barbarous country he withdrew and fixed his Roman eagle here. Our English Caesars then outshone the Roman, for Edward Longshanks passed the Tay and rifled Scone Abbey. But when history says he penetrated the remotest parts, I believe that means the parts then known to the English. Of Lochaber, Ross, Moray, Sutherland and Caithness we read nothing. From these vast retreats the Scots always returned with double strength after every setback and defeat. That is why Lord Protector Cromwell built citadels and forts at Inverness, Inverlochy and other points between, to contain the Highland fastness. King William reinforced these bulwarks and even the ferry routes into the western islands. Though he came not as a foreigner or conqueror but as a lawful governor and father of the people to whom he brought deliverance from slavery and oppression.

My dear Isobel, please forgive these musings, but standing as I am on the boundary of this great wilderness I feel its fearful extent, its unknown heights and the hidden threat of its peopled glens and dales. Might barbarian hordes still pour across these barely guarded

frontiers, amply armed with claymore and musket?
Could foreign enemies exploit the ancient allegiance
of these tribes to our exiled kings? This is what makes
the union of our nations so pressing and so much to be
desired.

Look, now I have rehearsed a new paper for the
press. I know that you will share my trepidations and
misgivings but it cannot be right for me to presume upon
your courtesy to such an extent. I stand rebuked for
intruding political matter into private correspondence.
Even more for omitting what is graceful and civilised
in your Scottish cities. I do not have apt gifts but I am
deeply sensible of the feminine influence. I am a plain
man of business and should stick to my allotted path of
duty in this earthly journey.

For now I am well situated in Dundee, a pleasant and
populous city more deserving of the epithet 'bonny' than
its unfortunate adventurer. I am told that of a lady in a
song 'bonny' signifies beautiful.

Tomorrow I leave for Aberdeen and then travel on to
Inverness. Whether I shall venture further into the wastes
is undecided. Already my thoughts are turning south to
Edinburgh, as if to home. I send my best compliments to
you, and to Mrs MacConnachie, if she is still with you in
that house by the Netherbow,

Most sincerely yours,

Daniel Foe

My dear Nellie,

I cannot tell you how much you have relieved my mind. There are few things in life that cannot be improved by a heart-to-heart talk with your oldest friend. And as you are well aware, and in fact predicted, my visit to Boness was most satisfactory. Until you remarked it, I had not seen this renewed address as preparation for a final parting, a settlement, as it were, of our affair. Perhaps this will be a year of conclusions and decisions, but so much remains uncertain. I write short as I have another invitation by messenger from Kinneil. Mr Foe continues in the north, writing in full measure.

With all my heartfelt thanks, my dearest Nellie, till we meet again,

Your own,
Isobel

I travelled by boat to Newcastle and then on to Montrose

alongside a cargo of coal. By agreement we knew nothing of the other's movements. Arriving at Glamis the next day I found the castle partly closed up and my Lord in Edinburgh. When I asked for Lady Glamis, the servant looked at me strangely as if I were out of the news, but offered no further information than that Lady Glamis was not at home. So I turned for Edinburgh. It was a poor beginning.

All around me were the scenes of boyhood and youth, alive with the colours of summer. I hired a horse to ride south, avoiding the ferries, but my emotions were disengaged and my mind elsewhere as I marked the stages of my journey, crossing the Tay at Perth and changing horses beneath the citadel of Stirling. Abruptly rampant from the level carse, Stirling Castle guards the upper reaches of the Forth and access to the Lowlands. On I went, past Bannockburn, Falkirk and Linlithgow Palace till I was clattering into the Grassmarket. I left my horse at the White Hart Inn and asked directions for the Canongate.

I found Lord Glamis much changed. The narrow face had tightened across his bones. The eyes were cold and piercing; he seemed tense and ambivalent, though I was expected. His greetings were courteous but somewhat perfunctory for such an old connection of his family; I felt the ghost of his mother passing, the spirit of an older, kindlier time.

Officially I had been engaged as his private secretary but I soon discovered that he kept any political communications to himself, treating me more as a priest and confessor. When he realised that I was not myself the bearer of secret dispatches he seemed relieved and advised me to say nothing of that business, even between

97

ourselves. Edinburgh, he claimed, had become a den of spies and schemers.

When not engaged in my light secretarial duties, I walked back and forth across the city till every street and wynd became familiar. All the time I scanned the passing faces in the hope of sighting Lady O'Kelly in some new role or disguise. I also went several times to Leith to watch the ships coming to and fro; they would be our best means of escape if things turned out badly for us.

On one of my many expeditions I finally saw her, by St Giles Church. Though she was modestly dressed, her looks were unmistakable and drew admiring glances. What kind of secret mission could she accomplish? Yet the attention she attracted to her sex and beauty could itself mislead. I followed her at a distance to an old High Street house just above the Netherbow Port. From then on I watched for her and was eventually rewarded with a curt nod of recognition. I cannot now recall whether that was before or after my dismissal.

I have described Lord Glamis as calculating in every motion. I sensed a ruthlessness in his nature, a cold steel before which it appeared Lady Glamis had gradually withdrawn, leaving her husband to his own devices. This I pieced together obliquely from his confessions and from casual remarks made by servants in the house.

But the picture as I have drawn it could mislead. To religion his suppressed emotions were attracted and sought release. His confessions were intense and his penances severe, needing my restraint and not my urging. At mass his ardour was wholehearted and apparent. To begin with I saw this as a link with his dear late mother, whose memory I always honoured in our prayers, but gradually I discerned another impulse. Reluctantly at first but then more clearly, I perceived the unnatural desire which he harboured. I tried resolutely to focus on my ministries and avoided his disturbing gaze.

The Union debate was dragging on day after day in Parliament. No determination seemed in prospect, though Glamis consistently maintained the anti-Union cause in all his speeches and discussions. Then without warning I was turned from the door of his Canongate mansion. This was my first crisis, for he might have betrayed me. But I judged that his main concern was to play safe and maintain distance between himself and one who could be exposed at any moment. It was also a clear warning that his final moves were undecided. Yet I did not panic or turn tail. I might be a priest but Murray blood still ran in my veins!

How can I explain these weeks and months even to myself? It was as if everything that had gone before was make-believe. Suddenly I was alive in every nerve and muscle, animated by a cause that seemed then to me more vital than even the principles of true religion.

Going straight to Leith, I enquired for lodgings and quickly found them from the landlord of the Ship Inn. It was a single room up an alley right beside the inn, close to the waterfront, discreet and cheap. I had little money left since the St Germain plan presumed on financial support from Glamis, but I had my own wit to fall back on. With my few remaining guineas I bought canvas, oils, crayon and brushes from an Edinburgh trader. The skills of draughtsmanship and painting had been nurtured at the seminary had now to be my means of livelihood. I set up as a jobbing artist and in this guise frequented the taverns and coffee houses of the town in search of business and of news.

In my new identity I sought out Lady O'Kelly to alert

her to the change of plan, contriving a chance encounter. We arranged to meet before the curfew at Trinity Chapel near the Netherbow, as if paying our respects to this ancient edifice. There, in a hurried twilight, I learnt of her success in contacting Hamilton through an old acquaintance. A private audience had been promised and I was engaged to be her guide to Holyrood, where, as hereditary keeper of the palace, the Duke had his town residence in state. That appointment was kept but with no more decisive result than my stay with Glamis. Everybody wished to be on the winning side, but which side might that be? The London mails were bringing poor news of Queen Anne's health.

On the night of the great negotiation debate, I was in the Grassmarket at the White Hart. I had been told that those of Covenanting inclinations often gathered there, and had been instructed to make some appraisal of the anti-Union factions. In addition, the Hart had proved an excellent place for picking up sign-painting work and an occasional portrait commission from some Edinburgh merchant who wanted to display his wife or daughter. The streets and taverns were full as if it were a market afternoon, and messengers came on the hour from Parliament.

It was already growing late, and though I had garnered one name, a Colonel Kennedy, I had not actually spoken to anyone from the southwest. I was gathering up my satchel and canvas when a growl or low ugly moan seemed to arise spontaneously and pass through the square. I hurried out in time to see a tide of bodies moving up the West Bow towards Parliament Hall.

'What is it?' I asked the nearest bystander.

'The Queen's men are pit doon tae London.'

Not only had the Scots Parliament voted to treat for Union but they had asked Queen Anne to appoint their

Commissioners for the negotiations. Unbelievably, this course of action had been proposed by Hamilton, supposed leader of the patriotic party. As another observed in his own Scots, 'It's aa lowsit, forbye the spillin o the ink.' Was this a great Hamilton betrayal, or a brilliant manoeuvre whose results were still to be discerned?

I followed the swell of people anxious to see the outcome. The mood was angry and threatening to turn violent. The crowd was densely ranked around Parliament and St Giles, intent on exacting some price from those who had sold Scotland so cheaply. My own thoughts turned to Catherine, still Lady O'Kelly to me. Was she safe, or had she been betrayed and trapped in this moment of unexpected reverse? With a sustained effort of shoving and pulling at packed bodies, I managed to cut down into the Cowgate and along towards the Netherbow. Behind me I heard the rage of the mob rise up and break like a great wave on the town's most ancient and symbolic buildings.

The windows of the house were all shuttered with a glow of candle light behind. Was she then secure in her lodgings? Some instinct or suspicion guided me past Leith Wynd and down the Canongate. A last late coach was standing outside the White Horse Inn at the Abbey Sanctuary. In the shadow of the inn wall a familiar figure stood forlornly beside her baggage, waiting to see if there would be space. I stepped forward into the lamplight and placed my hand on her arm. She started and then I saw the fear in her eyes turn to relief and welcome.

'Aeneas!'

'Come with me,' I urged quietly. 'You must not leave tonight.'

'Everything is lost, ruined.'

I drew her apart from the other travellers.

'Not necessarily. Have you been betrayed?'

'I don't know. I don't think so.'

'Then come with me till we see what can be tried.'

Her hand came into mine. Our eyes met for a short second. I hoisted up the trunk and we turned away from White Horse Close and started walking along the Watergate towards the road for Leith.

ॐ ॐ ॐ

My dear Mrs Rankin,

I had your mail safely in Aberdeen and I have now established camp at Inverness. Outside my window is a stately stone bridge of seven arches over the River Ness. By this bridge you enter what is truly the north of Scotland, or what some call the north Highlands. This frightful country is all one undistinguished range of mountains and woods overspread with vast and uninhabited rocky steeps filled with innumerable deer. Our geographers seem as much at a loss to describe this part of Scotland as the Romans were to conquer it, so they are obliged to fill it up with hills as they do the inner parts of Africa with elephants and lions. However it is not so difficult to access. I am busy exploring this country and will describe it for my readers in the following dispatches.

There are prodigious forests on all this land, reaching from ten to twenty miles in length, with fir trees large enough to make masts for the biggest of ships in the Royal Navy. Yet they are rendered useless for want of water carriage to bring them away. When I return to Edinburgh I must prepare a memorandum for the Parliament Committee. If Scots noblemen cannot fell the timber and cut it into masts and planks, they could burn it and extract immense quantities of pitch, tar and resin, which are of easier carriage and can be brought by horse to the water's edge. This way their woods may be made profitable.

To give an account of religion in these parts is an unpleasant work. You would hardly believe that in a Christian island as this is said to be there should be people who know so little of true belief as to confuse a Sabbath with a working day, or worship from a pagan celebration. It is to be hoped that after the Union means will be found to redress this calamitous situation. Funds must be gathered, in London as well as Edinburgh, so that the General Assembly may send ministers and missionaries, for propagation of the Gospel is an urgent task in these northern regions and a needful charity. In time by God's grace such horrible ignorance will be dispelled.

Anything these poor abandoned wretches know of God, living as they do in poverty as well as ignorance, any glimpse they have of light is by the diligence of Popish clergy. The priests have taken more pains to remedy their defects than those from whom this work should have been expected. I write this for your eyes only because it has affected me so strongly and because I know your own sense and spirit.

If truth be told, my mind is now set on Edinburgh. Your kindness in reserving my room has been a steady anchor through these wanderings. In three days I shall be again at Aberdeen and then turn southwards to safe harbour.

I look forward to renewing our conversations face to face. Our friendship arises from the mutual esteem and respect which only those who have seen something of the world can share in their maturer age.

I am most cordially,
Your own,
Daniel Foe

What you are about to read forms no part of my memoir;

it will lie apart, sealed among my papers. Perhaps in fifty, sixty or a hundred years, who knows, someone will care to try and piece together the fragments of inner truth which comprise a so-called turning point in our affairs. Sometimes, even in my own mind these months seem like a dream, a chapter out of time.

I will continue the main narrative with my return to St Germain leading on to the tragic endeavour of 1715. That was the last time I saw my beloved Scotland, touched her earth and breathed her air. Yet as I write, the young Prince has landed in the Western Isles to raise the standard once again. God grant him fair speed. But I must remain calm here in the seminary where I am so well looked after in my frail age. What would the students think of their venerable old teacher if these pages were spread before them?

When we arrived in Leith, Catherine, as I now must call her, was in a state of shock and exhaustion. I lit a fire to warm the small room. She unlaced and stepped out of her elegant gown. As she stood shivering in a cotton shift I wrapped her in my blankets and she climbed into the recessed bed. Though I heated a toddy of cheap whisky, she wanted neither drink nor speech and fell soundlessly into a deep sleep. I sat by the fire for the rest of the night in our only chair.

In the morning she awoke refreshed. I looked away while she dug in her trunk to find a plain woollen dress and a dark shawl, the garb of a better off peasant. We had some bread and milk from my small store and took counsel.

I pressed my argument that Hamilton's apparent betrayal might be a tactic to force rebellion on the part of a majority. If the terms of Union were unacceptable to Scotland, as they surely would be in a one-sided negotiation, then a rising would become inevitable. Catherine accepted this, perhaps over-readily. Our aim therefore was to maintain contact and so enable a flow of information amongst those sympathetic to the cause, and in particular the safe delivery of any secret dispatches on military dispositions, equipment and money.

This moment disclosed the bond of trust that had been formed by our common trial and danger. Catherine revealed that she was the bearer of these dispatches, but that apart from the letter already given to Hamilton she had not yet received any specific instructions about their delivery. I realised that she must be the emissary whom Glamis expected and feared, and seized on this as proof that we must stay to carry through our mission. But in my heart I knew that these papers put us both in deadly danger. Nor, following my breach with Glamis, did either of us know how or by whom these dispositions should be received. Notwithstanding, we quickly formed a plan of action.

I would give out to the landlord and his sociable spouse that my wife had arrived to share the meagre living of a jobbing artist. They turned out to be kindness itself, providing us with more blankets, a fireside stool and pots with hooks for cooking over the fire. The landlord and his lady were ideal social guarantors, since, informed by them of our situation, people accepted us without question or suspicion.

Catherine began to play the wife, going out to market, washing and hanging linen on a line above the back court. This, she joked, was a new role for her, but she was soon established among the Leith folk who were both warm and ready with a word of jest or practical advice at every turn. Despite the busy come and go of ships, Catherine was rarely troubled by sailors or carriers. She wore her beauty modestly and going out to shop, wrapped herself in a plain shawl. She almost looked like a nun.

Each day I walked up to Edinburgh with my paints and canvas. My services came to be in constant demand. Every merchant in the town seemed to want a likeness recorded. Was it that people sensed a moment of change and wished to mark it in some tangible way? I did not need to advertise my wares but attended at the taverns to gather messages and the general news.

I did, however, frequent the Canongate, calling at the great mansions to present my respects and services. Many of the nobility were in London and the Glamis town-house remained unrelentingly closed. Nevertheless, I did receive some commissions, including the instruction to paint Queensberry's wife. The lady seemed wan and sad, and I learned from the servants that in the upper regions of that great house her oldest son, the young Marquis, was strictly confined, a slavering lunatic. That was the second time I had glimpsed misery behind the facade of a great man's life. No word of a conclusion or even progress arrived from the southern capital to interrupt my labours.

Each evening I returned to Leith. A simple meal would be ready for me there, usually fish, or sometimes mutton cooked as a stew and served with coarse bread to mop up the juices. Whisky was plentiful in Leith but with my success we were able to buy claret from the Ship, and on some grand occasions we had beef or venison roasted in the great open fire of the inn kitchen. After supper I would organise my paints and brushes for the next day's work. Catherine would take up some sewing or embroidery. Often we just sat either side of the fire and talked.

It began naturally enough. One night Catherine was

telling me about her life with the Chevalier O'Kelly. She had met him first in Edinburgh, and of course owed her part in our employment to that knowledge of the town. But she explained that their union had been unhappy. I knew O'Kelly only slightly as one of the wilder set at St Germain. Catherine confirmed his drunkenness and gambling, hinting gently at worse. She spoke of the shameful resorts to which she had been driven for their survival. She was upset and tense so I held her in my arms to soothe and comfort. Soon we lay down together.

That first time we only clung to each other through the night, but from then on we came together as man and wife. There was no shame in this relation. We were a man and woman thrown together by the force of hostile circumstance; from these simple acts of love we drew mutual strength and comfort. Adam and Eve did not blush in the Garden until the serpent introduced a guilty imputation.

That was the beginning, but as the weeks of summer passed into autumn, so my love became a passion. I wanted to see and touch every part of her, to contain her in all my senses. I began to sketch and paint Catherine, though this provoked our only quarrel. When Catherine saw her beautiful body appearing on my canvas in all its naked glory she denied me outright. I protested that her beauty was my inspiration. She took the canvas and the preparatory sheets, and threw them in the fire. Then there were unusual floods of tears and I consoled her, but I never attempted to record her likeness again. Until now.

It was a few days after this that Catherine began to tell me the truth of her upbringing in Edinburgh. Of course I had already recounted my childhood and muddled origins. While she spoke she looked not at me but steadily into the fire, relating all in an impassive tone, even to the three times that some old howdie had poisoned a baby in her womb before it could grow to full life. When the recital was complete she rose without a further word and rolled herself up in our blankets as on the first night that she had come to Leith. I stared into the fire, trying to relive some of what she had told me. Then I rose and climbed in beside her and held her passive form firmly in my arms through the hours of darkness.

We were alike, I told her the next morning, never having known Paradise. We had come through hell but now we were dwelling in an Eden created by our own love. She called me priest but blushed with pleasure and took me back to bed.

Then suddenly the treaty was concluded. Rumour had it that the two sides had not met face to face, the Scots commissioners sitting apart in an antechamber and received drafts dictated by the English party. Now the terms were to be studied and debated by the two Parliaments. The time for waiting had expired. Within a week of this news reaching Edinburgh a servant stopped me in the Canongate and summoned me to attend on Glamis.

The interview was brief. He barely looked at me, but commanded me to leave Scotland immediately, saying he could no longer answer for my safety. I objected that my mission was not complete till I knew that all the dispatches had been delivered.

His reply was swift as if he had anticipated this point. 'Tell your emissaries, whoever they might be, to speak with Colonel Kennedy of Ballintrae.' He would make no further comment on this issue.

I pressed him on his own loyalty to the cause. I had never challenged Glamis before but the memory of his devoted mother gave me courage. When I invoked her name his narrow lip twisted in a snarl. 'Don't presume, priestling. Even my family's famous generosity has its limits. Take that for your pains.' He was clutching a leather pouch and threw it onto the table. Some coins spilled out, rolled round and fell flat one after another with a dull metallic clatter. We both stared.

'Take your wages and go.'

'Keep your silver pieces. You may yet earn them.'

A hand went to his side, but I was already turning and I strode out of his house into the buzz of the street, then kept walking.

I knew I had behaved foolishly. Who could say what double game he was now engaged in and at what risk to our survival? Yet time was to prove my instinct true. Meanwhile I had put myself in further danger. Would he hunt me out and have me killed? Or hand me to the government in Scotland? Could he do that without betraying his own part? Or had he already traded that in return for some advantage?

I returned to Leith by the Watergate, the long way round. My unexpected arrival surprised Catherine at her daily washing, arms submerged in a wooden tub of clothes. At that moment the rhythm of our private Eden was broken.

Catherine was calm as she absorbed my news and decisive in response. I must go by ship to France. She would stay to see it out, following up on the name of Colonel Kennedy. I begged her to come with me but she was resolute. I demanded why? What could she set against our love?

She smiled sadly and took me in her arms. 'You are a priest,' she said. 'I am a courier and a married whore. This cannot last.'

I felt the cold shock of that but urged my case. How could she succeed here alone?

She said she would go back to Mrs Rankin's lodgings. As she herself was in no immediate danger, Lady O'Kelly could renew connections. With those words a shadow fell between us.

'Please, please come away.'

'It's too late now.' She shook her head as she moved apart from me and tears began. 'I have nothing to go back for. Paradise cannot be regained.'

These were her last words.

When I came back from the quay her old finery was spread out on the bed. But when we walked out and stood embracing on the quay the woollen dress and black habit were her only garments. As darkness fell and the boat slipped its moorings, moving out to catch the tide, she had already disappeared, swallowed up into the wynds and closes of the port. I gazed back towards the dulled lights and dusky smoke of Edinburgh. They seemed to burn in my soul like an inferno.

PART THREE

'The Treaty goes to Parliament next week. This barbarous

country is already in uproar.' The letter was held at a distance from Reid's body as if infectious or at the least distasteful. 'I cannot vouch for what may happen in the streets when the members vote it through.'

'Is this a new uproar or continuation of the old?' Harley was bibbed and tuckered at the mirror and impatient not to displace his early morning rituals.

'Reports frae Paris, Dieppe, Dublin.' Reid continued briskly. 'The Continent is quiet and Ireland peaceable. The talk in Edinburgh is of rebellion.'

'Is that Foe's account? Shave me as you talk.'

Reid began to apply the soap, lathering methodically.

'Last time a French ship sailed up the Forth there wisna eneuch pouder tae fire one cannon at her.'

'He's inclined to hysterics is he not?'

'Wee touch excitable, but no necessarily wrang.' Reid took the razor in his right hand, stropped, and began to draw it down over Harley's stubbled double chin.

'So what's his actual news?'

'The Kirk's declared a Day o Fast an Humiliation agin the Union.'

'You Scots know how to make merry.' Harley almost smiled but remembered in time not to wobble his chins.

'He says the Hielans may rise. They're a law untae theirsels, onyroads.'

'Then we have war. It's convenient that we left Scotland without an army of its own, but a nuisance if troops have to be withdrawn from Europe.'

Reid submerged the razor in a basin of warm soapy water. It emerged pristine. 'The Jacobites an Covenanters have sworn tae staun by ane anither. According to Mr Foe.'

'Who could broker such a strange marriage?'

'That's exactly whit Foe should find oot. Instead o aa

this useless scribbling.' Harley flinched. 'There's aye some bodie ready tae tak up airms in Scotland.' Reid moved seamlessly from cheek to jaw to throat.

'North and South may unite to sting.' Harley was enjoying the smooth warmth. 'But without a leader the sting is drawn.'

'Aye, if Hamilton bides at hame a wee tuilzie micht distract attention an flush oot the troublemakers.' Reid rinsed off the remaining soap.

'Do you suggest we provoke a rebellion in Her Majesty's realm of Scotland? You surprise me, sir. But we do have a useful connection in the southwest.'

'Foe's trying the Covenanters as weill.'

'He's no fool, though impractical at times.'

'Is he no oot o his depth wi rebellions?' Reid laid down the razor, and Harley offered his chin for drying.

'That feels good. You're right. Armed revolt may not be in Mr Foe's line, but he might still be useful. Playing the traitor from devotion to duty will tease his devious low church conscience with delight. No offence of course to religious principle.'

'Aye.' Reid began to tidy up, closing the razor with a snap. Harley sat back, contentedly waiting for his wig.

'What do you really think about this Union, William?'

'It's no my place to think.'

'William.'

'I don't like it. They're sellin oor birthright.'

'But to Scotland's advantage.'

'Maybe. We're slittin oor ain throats wi oor eyes open. I'll cast oot the slops.' Harley was left to his own thoughts.

༒ ༒ ༒

There was a comfortable silence in the parlour by the

Netherbow. They sat on either side of the fire, sipping claret and contemplating the coals crumbling in the hearth.

'It's very quiet.'

'Calm before the storm.'

'Trade is suffering.'

'Without doubt.'

'But the final session of Parliament will draw them back in.'

'Final session? So you believe the Union Treaty will be approved?'

'Parliament will vote for it. You know that.'

'There might be a war.'

'God forbid, Daniel. When I was a wee lass we lived in never-ending fear of war and rebellion. It was a way of life.'

'Where was that?'

'In Midlothian, beside the Moorfoot Hills.'

'You were a country girl – sorry – lass?'

'Not really. Dalkeith is a small town. There were mines and mills, but when hard times came people used to leave for Edinburgh.'

'Is that how you came here, Isobel?'

'No. I was drawn to Edinburgh by the idea of wealth, and the glamour of a big town.' A wistful smile passed over her face but Foe missed it.

'Was that not a vain deceit?'

'Are you not drawn to London?'

'I love it and detest it with the same breath. London is my true home but I have spent most of my life having to leave it.' It was Foe's turn to smile. 'You married in Edinburgh?'

Isobel hesitated for a second. 'I experienced what Edinburgh had to give a young woman without family or connections.'

'A young attractive woman.'

'Once perhaps. That was long since before I was widowed.'

'Like Lady Catherine.'

'I can honestly say that I never lived in the same way as she does.'

Foe sensed Isobel's withdrawal. 'She left us in a great hurry. For Ireland.'

'Daniel, I am not sure that she went to Ireland.'

'Why not?'

'She is a woman in love with risk and danger.'

'Yet you tried to protect her, Isobel. I detected a mother's tenderness in your feelings for her.'

'I never had a daughter or a son. But you are right, I did want to protect her.'

'You think she may be living dangerously?'

'I don't really know but I am sure that she has not told us the whole truth of her business in Edinburgh.' Isobel looked directly at Foe.

'These are difficult times in Scotland,' he proffered. 'Things may get worse before they get better. The Scots are passionate and patriotic.'

'It's no longer possible to be a spectator. The future of our country is being decided. But these disputes must not be allowed to turn into a war.'

'I salute you as a woman of sense.' Foe raised his glass.

'I learned early not to betray my heart in a harsh world.' The toast was not reciprocated. 'I am a widow, Daniel, living in quiet circumstances, and that is what I must remain.'

'You can depend on my discretion.'

'And you on mine.'

Relaxed silence was restored and the two gazed thoughtfully into the fire from their respective positions.

የታየታ

'Colonel Kennedy.'

The voice, low and strangely soft, came out of the shadows. Kennedy peered into a dark passageway leading down from the courtyard to the stables.

'Please step aside into this corner.' The voice had moved away from the passage and Kennedy followed it.

'Who are you?'

'Lady O'Kelly of Balnacross.'

'From Ireland?'

'I come to you as a loyal servant of the crown.'

'A woman. Are you mad?' All Kennedy could make out was a tall figure. The face was veiled.

'In some circumstances a woman attracts less attention.'

'Not in a tavern yard at night.' Kennedy scanned the courtyard again but it seemed to be empty.

'This place is not my choice. I have to be ready to travel at any moment.'

'Do you have the papers?' As his eyes adjusted to the gloom, Kennedy scoured the ground for any evidence of baggage.

'They are safely lodged with friends of our cause. We need to be sure of your intentions.' The veiled woman neither drew nearer nor gave way.

'Why should I explain myself to you? My name and my sword are more than sufficient guarantees.'

'Not in France.'

'The Covenanters need to know that the North will rise and that French assistance will arrive. When they have assurance on these counts through me they will rise, as they have done many times before.'

'Everything you require is laid out in the papers – numbers, dispositions, pledges of men and money from the French Government.'

'Good. But I must show these directly to the leading men. They are not over-trusting when it comes to Papish promises.'

'I myself will bring everything to you in Edinburgh. But you must find somewhere secure to meet.'

'Are you being followed?' With one sudden reach of a massive arm, Kennedy had her hard against the wall.

'No. I have stayed out of town.'

'You've done well.' As Catherine held her nerve, Kennedy released his grip and took a step back. 'Not many women could carry it off. Where are you lodging?'

'Nearby.'

'Let me take you there.'

She could smell his breath and sweat. 'We must leave as if this were a chance encounter. Now.'

Kennedy stepped aside. 'When do we next meet?'

'I will get another note to you with the place and time.'

'Don't leave it for long. The godly are in heat and need to be served now.'

'Not tonight, sir.' She was moving again towards the passage. 'I have other gentlemen waiting.'

'Damn you.'

Suddenly she was gone.

శౄశౄశౄ

The page is pure and blank. Why mark it? Blots. Smudges.

Black ink stains white paper.

I hold my hands pressed flat upon the table. I do not want to turn back these pages. They are entries in someone else's hand. Some other journal. My line has been drawn since Aeneas took his departure. The sheet is clean.

There is no further need to think. Just act. Shut the book. I am Glamis and that duty prevails, let pleasure take where it will.

It has lain quietly and safely for months, locked and sealed from sight. Now it lies ready on my table, anonymous and bound. Ready for the fire. Because Glamis knows his own will.

Unlike the Duke of Dithers. He claims his right but I hold everything in my decision. To have and hold, at my command.

Without intimacy or confession. Place my hand on the closed book. There, no remembrance or recall.

Is it not within my power to keep? For my eyes alone. My own book safe and unopened.

Time yet to burn.

❧❧❧

Queensberry and Glamis sat together in an antechamber

of the Marquis' imposing residence in the Canongate. Rumour had it that even the royal house had resented the way in which Queensberry's grand belvedere overlooked Holyrood Palace. The grate was empty and cold but they sat before it in elegant, upright chairs. Their mutual antagonism had drained away, though it had not been replaced by cordiality or warmth.

The formal business began.

'Some action may be inevitable after Parliament votes the treaty through.' Queensberry's delivery was flat and even.

'Not our action, I hope. The Scottish garrison is bereft of supplies and of command.'

'Did I say our action?' Muscles moved beneath the Queensberry's bland features. 'The English government commands Scottish regiments.'

Both men reached for the glasses of Madeira which had been placed on the table between them. Glamis noted Queensberry's new London purchases with interest.

'If the Highlands rise,' he intoned, 'we will have war.'

'But wars need leaders,' countered Queensberry.

They sipped appreciatively. Glamis sampled the nuts and raisins that were set out on a silver salver.

'I am dining with the Duke tonight,' resumed the host. 'They say he has taken up again with an old liaison that detains him at Kinneil.'

'The Prince of bastards, mated with the Queen of whores.'

'Do I detect a note – the tiniest whiff – of pique?' Queensberry scooped up his own handful of nuts and raisins.

'My tastes lie elsewhere.'

'You intrigue me. What do you recommend for an ageing

Presbyterian, apart from the Committee of Trade?'

'Surely that doesn't have to meet again? The treaty goes before Parliament in the next few days.'

'Precisely.' Queensberry was unbending. 'But you and I, Glamis, constitute a special sub-committee to finalise the monetary detail.'

'God, how I hate this veneer of business. Yet I suppose we must ensure our financial protection.'

'We are to enjoy a private audience with a good English tradesman.'

Before Glamis could muster a sneer, the wooden screens opened and Foe was ushered in, wearing his best dress coat and powdered wig. He stood uncertainly in the gap.

'You are most welcome, Mr Foe,' said Queensberry, without rising.

At this, Foe came forward to a table in the centre of the room, bearing an armful of papers.

'Please use the table,' invited Queensberry, coming to his feet, 'for your papers and...'

'Weights, your lordship.'

'Of course, weights. Glamis, will you...?'

'My Lord Glamis.'

Glamis rose to take his place at the table, while Foe arranged his materials at the other side. Then, like an actor surveying his scene before the curtain rises, the merchant of London checked his props and began his address.

'Properly understood, this treaty is a coalition founded on equalities and equivalents. No-one can object to something so intrinsically just.'

'But everyone who has drunk the elixir of monetary wisdom,' objected Glamis, unwilling to cede the principle, 'contests that Scots trade will be damaged.'

'When the present interests of the two kingdoms clash,' explained Foe stolidly, 'an equivalent will be paid.'

'An equivalent?' questioned Glamis.

'All matters of value can be made good through some transaction – even life or honour.'

'Mend virginity and I'm your man.'

The peculiar muscular motion rippled from mouth to ear across Queensberry's face. 'Come to the point, Mr Foe.'

'My Lord. As you know, Scots losses in customs duties will be compensated by a once-and-for-all payment.'

'While further monies will be at the disposal of Scotland to recompense those it judges to have lost most. An admirable principle.' Glamis was on more familiar territory here.

'We have objected to some of the details of the customs arrangements,' added Queensberry, 'but through Foe's good offices a final revised draft will go to London.'

'And be accepted?'

'Mr Foe has argued for flexibility.' Queensberry reached across for a paper.

'Then Mr Foe is in fact a friend.'

'My aim, Lord Glamis, is to settle here in Scotland and establish a glassmaking factory.'

'How fascinating. That should compensate for all the Scots who will now take up residence in London.'

'This is excellent, Foe.' Queensberry was deep in the detail. 'The corn bounty will be extended to barley. For the purposes of fish curing, English salt will be treated like foreign salt. There is a flat rate of six shillings and eightpence to the bushel.'

'What is a bushel?' enquired Glamis in disbelief.

'Eighty-four pounds.' This from Foe. 'The system

already operates in England.'

'My God, I can almost smell fish. What about these magical equivalents? How much is envisaged?'

'The loss to Scotland is valued at four hundred thousand pounds.'

'A handsome sum.' Glamis reclined against the stiff back of his chair.

Queensberry was less impressed by this enormous total. 'Have you reckoned the overall balance of trade?'

'I have abridged the main heads,' responded Foe, warming to his theme. As he spoke, he deftly allocated weights to two neatly stacked piles. 'See on this side the exports to England: oats, cattle, sheep, salt, coals, wool and fish. On this side, the debits: household goods, clothes, ships, horses, coaches, and jewels. If Scotland applies herself to improving manufactures, you will have the balance by three hundred thousand pounds per annum.' This was clearly demonstrated, with one pile now higher than the other.

'What will the gentry and nobility spend in London?' probed Glamis.

'The Court is already there,' parried Foe, 'but I have allowed fifty thousand pounds.'

'How do you explain the present decay in trade?' Queensberry took up a point that had been raised by Glamis in Parliament.

'The lack of advantageous conditions,' declared Foe confidently. 'We are creating the largest area of free trade in Europe. If the nobility apply some of the money they get in England to Scotland, then the people will prosper.'

'But the people want no part in your Union, Mr Foe'. This was stated with Glamis' normal ironic detachment but it had a flavour of conviction.

'What have they to fear? Their condition cannot be worse than what they experience now. Take the wool trade. If your stewards employed the people to spin the wool into yarn –'

'Enough.' Glamis came to his feet. 'You will turn noblemen into merchants of your own kind. I must leave you to your tract.'

Foe's chair scraped in his haste to get up. 'I am honoured to have met you.'

'Will you be at the late sitting?' Queensberry had also risen.

'You can count on it.' Then he was gone. The other two resumed their places.

'The details of management are not to his lordship's taste.' Queensberry condescended. 'How is your other business proceeding? This bond between the Jacobites and the Covenanters is gaining ground.'

'I am preparing an urgent address to Glasgow, scorning that Presbyterians and Papists should bed together.'

'On instructions from London?'

'For our mutual interest.'

'Good.' This seemed to satisfy Queensberry. 'We must drive a wedge between them.'

'I am working constantly towards that end. Can I rely on you to commend my efforts to Her Majesty?'

'You want me to recommend your service?' The Marquis was genuinely surprised.

'Only those who govern can commend a secret service.'

'That is true, Mr Foe, and you are serving two governments at the same time. I for my part will endeavour to apply your services to good effect.'

'I am in your debt.' Foe gathered up his papers and

began to back out through the doors which had been left open by Glamis. 'Good afternoon, your lordship.'

'When the park is finished, I will lay out a garden. It is the fashion in London.'

Isobel was on Hamilton's arm, looking down a grassy incline towards the Firth of Forth, which gleamed gold under the setting sun. The stream of evening light came low over the classically solid house to glance off the surface of the river onto the hills beyond.

'You have a fine view.'

'That is true, but the garden must be laid out in front where the main road approaches.' Hamilton's nightshirt waved in protest at his formality of manner, the freshening evening breeze blowing around his legs despite the long cloak wrapped around his shoulders. His shaven head was bare.

'What are all these ruins?' Isobel's focus had switched to the mossy, uneven foreground.

'At one time the people lived there,' replied Hamilton with a dismissive wave. 'They were removed when the park was first enclosed.' The jagged walls and gaping windows of a church stood amidst the detritus of cottages and outhouses.

'Nothing endures, even at Kinneil.' She drew a woollen wrap more tightly round her shoulders.

'You are melancholic.'

'Do you blame me?'

'I am often melancholic when I consider the fortunes of my House. My ancestors were the Dukes of Chatelrault. Now I must beg my mother for money.'

'She is the Duchess of Hamilton in her own right. You have your wife's estates.'

'They are my mainstay, Isobel. Without them I would be lost for ready money.'

'Not everyone has recourse to another's fortune.'

'But Lancashire is not convenient.' Hamilton turned

away impatiently to pace along his emergent terrace. 'My wife should be here at Kinneil. She ought to be mindful of how close I stand to the throne.'

Rooted to the spot, Isobel felt a sudden weight washing through her body and into her limbs. She had expected nothing else, yet this blatant confirmation of her irrelevance to Hamilton's nearest interests drained away any unacknowledged hopes.

'The times are out of joint and we must make the best of it,' she offered feebly.

'I am slighted at Court.' Hamilton was indignant.

'You could use your power to restore King James,' observed Isobel with cool logic.

'If I give Scotland to them, will I finally be rewarded?'

'To the English or the French?' Isobel was losing track. The Duke continued to pace.

'What do I care for the choice? I should have married you when we were young and lovers.'

The shock of this caught her unawares. She stepped back against the wall. 'Did you have a choice?' she managed to force out against her loss of breath.

'You were always my equal. A shared mind.'

'But we have kept faith in our own ways,' she consoled. 'Your confidence today has touched my feelings.' She moved towards Hamilton and reached out for his arm. 'What you have told me will go no further, but it may prevent harm to people I know and care for. I am in your debt in these testing times.'

Hamilton came to a halt and took Isobel's hand in his. 'You are the rock, my love, on which my melancholy foundered. The only thing on which my mind was set.'

The sincerity of this retrospect was almost unbearable. Isobel gently released her hand. 'Shall we take another turn around the house?' The evening cool seemed suddenly inviting.

'Its getting chilly. Let's go in,' vetoed Hamilton. 'I have a drawing of the new gates to show you.'

Isobel regained her composure. 'The avenue will be a credit to your house.'

'The price of land will rise. It is inevitable. We shall eat in my private apartments.'

'I should return to Edinburgh.'

'Tomorrow. Kinneil will always be open to you.'

'It is not my place to visit here.'

'You do me honour.' Hamilton caressed her arm and drew his own around her waist. 'Come in and we can be intimate together.'

'I must go home tomorrow.'

'You are the thing closest to my heart.'

'When I am forgotten,' she murmured into his shoulder, 'your part will always be remembered.' She surrendered to a warm embrace, suspending disbelief.

ఈఈఈ

Transferring her luggage by cart, Catherine spent two

nights at the White Hart. She informed the landlord that she was waiting for her brother and mother to arrive. It was noticeable how helpful people in Scotland were to an unaccompanied woman. French and Italian manners were very different in this regard, as in so many others.

Edinburgh was rapidly filling up in anticipation of the Parliament. The General Assembly of the Kirk was already in extraordinary session. Rooms were not easy to find, so on this pretext Catherine was able to scout the familiar streets and to keep an unobtrusive watch on the house by the Netherbow. A homespun cloak was enough to mask her bearing and identity.

She was rapidly using up the last of the money that Aeneas had left, but after two days her persistence was rewarded when she saw an anonymous coach draw up in the High Street, and Isobel Rankin slipping quietly out into this conveyance and away. Three or four times daily Mr Foe bustled out and in, papers and pamphlets under his arm. All pretence of privacy seemed to have gone; he appeared to be a man of affairs, at ease in Edinburgh and thrang with its business.

On the third afternoon since leaving Leith, Catherine had a cadie move her bags to the Netherbow and she climbed the steep external stair and entered the parlour. Foe rose in surprise if not astonishment.

'Lady Catherine!'

He was in full possession of the parlour, dressed only in a shirt and waistcoat, and rose suddenly from poring over a dishevelled table of papers.

'I... we... didn't expect...' A cotton hankie was wrapped around Foe's shaven and wigless head.

'I have made an unexpected return. Forgive my haste.'

'No, of course, you are very welcome. Please make

yourself at... have a seat.'

Catherine took the proffered seat. 'Where is Mrs Rankin?'

'I am sorry, she is away out of town at present but –'

'Is she at Kinneil?'

'I expect her home at any time. She will be surprised to see you back from Ireland.'

'But not necessarily pleased.'

'She will be concerned for you, of course. You seem tired. Can I pour you a glass of claret?'

'That would be very kind. Thank you. Please have a glass with me, Mr Foe. You are an amiable host.'

'Forgive my informality. I have become very used to this hospitable house.'

'Indeed.' Catherine sipped gratefully from her glass. 'Yet, my dear Mr Foe, you too look fatigued and hard-worked. Are you unwell?'

'No, thank God, I have a strong constitution.' Foe sank into the other fireside seat. 'But to be honest, my business here is not going well.'

'I am truly sorry to hear that. I have no wish to pry...'

'You are very circumspect. But there is no need for discretion when things are so public.'

'What is the trouble, Mr Foe?'

To such an appeal Foe was ready to confide. 'You know that I came to Edinburgh to try and set up a factory.'

'You told me something of the kind.' Catherine was all attention.

'But I had another purpose. My aim was to persuade people to the Union, and so advance my own enterprise. Being by religion a dissenter, I felt I might find a hearing in this Presbyterian nation.'

'Scotland has not conformed to your expectations. I

believe Mrs Rankin may have warned you not to expect too –'

'Yes, but this goes beyond the worst expectations.' Foe was bolt upright in his seat. 'Defiance has become a fever, a contagion. Last week, honest Glasgow was a scene of riot. Tradesmen took cause with Papist rebels against the Union.'

'That is the national mood. I sensed it immediately returning from Ireland.' Catherine was surprised by his burst of passion. 'You cannot blame yourself, Mr Foe.'

'Yet, madam, I have tried to press home the advantages at meetings and in print. My efforts will be accounted a failure.' Foe looked like a harassed, middle-aged man at home; the competent veneer had gone. The rehearsal of his trials seemed to have exhausted him.

'Yet they say,' Catherine hazarded in her most soothing tones, 'that Parliament will pass the Act of Union in the next few days.'

'Yes,' groaned Foe, 'along with special guarantees for the Kirk. But what will follow? A mass rebellion? This is the most ungovernable of nations,' he concluded glumly.

'Are your own prospects damaged by these reverses?'

'I believe I still have one last chance to achieve something – on my own account. A private communication.'

'You are a gambler, staking all on his last throw,' Catherine tried, suddenly attentive.

'A card sharp,' admitted Foe ruefully. 'You may be right.'

'Do not give way to depression. I know how debilitating it can be.' A sympathetic hand was stretched across the fire in Foe's direction.

'I am sorry. How distracting this must be when you have troubles of your own to contend with.'

'Can I speak honestly as you have done?'

'Lady O'Kelly, I would be honoured to be your confidante.'

'Please, call me Catherine.'

'Lady Catherine.'

'Mr Foe, my affairs are more desperate than I dared to hint before.'

'Your estate is exhausted?'

'Ruined. I've returned with the final hope of persuading my cousin's lawyers to release the entire legacy. Or throw myself on the mercy of my acquaintance.'

'God forbid.'

'I am at the end of my resources.'

'You must not despair. Help may be close at hand.' Foe's own hand was extended.

'Please, don't mock me with false comfort.' Catherine looked away.

'God's mercy is nearer than we dare think or believe. Don't make any rash undertaking – neither Mrs Rankin nor I could allow it.'

'What can you do?' Catherine's eyes engaged.

'Let me be a friend in adversity,' Foe responded.

'I could not accept your consolation lightly.'

'I shall show you firm evidence of my concern.'

'How could I repay such kindness?'

'Only by mutual affection and esteem. Your kindness is itself a favour.'

'Is that Isobel?' Steps could be heard on the stair.

'I don't think so.' Male voices were echoing up the turnpike in subdued tones. 'Please will you receive the visitors...' Foe gestured towards his tousled shirt and shaven head as he moved for the door.

'Of course. We will talk later.'

Foe slipped out, and as the door opened the visitors' last exchange reached the parlour.

'Would we no be better leevin aff?'

'Calm yersel, Archie. It's just a wee diversion from oor labours.'

'Good afternoon, gentlemen.' Catherine rose gracefully to receive the two black-coated ministers.

'Good afternoon. I'm not sure if I have been...'

'You seem surprised, Mr...'

'We were expecting –'

'Mrs Rankin.'

'Yes, indeed.'

'We kin pay oor respects anither day.' The Reverend Archie tugged at his colleague's coat sleeve.

'Please do not unsettle yourselves on my account.' Catherine indicated the two fireside seats and the ministers stiffly took their places.

'The wind's a touch snell for May,' ventured Archie.

''Enough to drive you indoors for comfort at any rate,' she agreed.

'Perhaps we should introduce ourselves,' the younger clergyman began.

'I dinna think that's aa thegither –'

'No necessity for introductions,' intervened Catherine smoothly. 'I see that you are known in the house, else the lassie would not have steered you up.'

'Of course. We are old acquaintances of Mrs Rankin. Even before I entered into my present vocation I knew her well. Where is the good lady of the house?'

'Mrs Rankin is in the country for a few days. I myself have just returned from Ireland,' Catherine remarked sociably.

'A fine country though a touch infected wi the Papist

sickness,' demurred Archie.

'There are worse infections.'

'I ne'er heard o them masel.'

'Then you are indeed fortunate.' Archie was ready to flee.

'You must forgive my friend,' smoothed the other. 'His thoughts are on his higher duties.'

'I understand,' consoled Catherine, 'the General Assembly must be very strenuous this year.'

'It's a sair fecht richt eneuch.'

'Feelings are running high,' confirmed the second minister.

'Quite so. Perhaps I could offer you a refreshment?'

'That would be very welcome.'

'But we think they'll be won roond at the last.'

'You surprise me. Are you permitted a glass of claret?'

'The true interests of the Kirk demand a Protestant Union. Thank you. But we must not weary you with our debates.'

'Aye. Much obleeged.'

'We all need some relief,' he sipped, 'from these contentions.'

Catherine sat on the edge of the carved settle.

'Mrs Rankin keeps a hospitable house,' continued the younger man.

'And so do I in her absence. That is what she expressly wishes.'

'I am glad to hear it.' The glass was drained.

'If you have time to take your ease I will provide some entertainment in Mrs Rankin's place.'

'I dinna play at cairtes. It's no seemly for a man o releegion.'

'Heaven forbid,' exclaimed Catherine, 'I had no

thought of gaming.'

'I'm sure my colleague…'

'Some other form of pleasure may be allowed. I am wholly in your hands, gentlemen, and would be content to fall in with your dispositions as with Mrs Rankin's. My only regret is that I am here today alone.'

'I see.'

'Perhaps some accommodation might be…' Catherine gestured towards the door and upper stair.

'There's nae rush.' Archie was on his feet. 'I'll wait for Isobel anither day.' He made for the door.

'You must excuse my colleague,' proffered the younger man, as he edged more subtly towards the door. 'He has a country parish.' The door swung behind him too.

For the first time since Aeneas had left, Catherine laughed out loud. Then she poured herself a full glass of claret.

❧❧❧

The coach rattled along steadily despite the bumps.

Although she had the blind drawn down on the coast side, Isobel Rankin paid little attention to the sunshine and cloudy shadows which were chasing each other across the Forth. Borrowstonness, the Binns, Abercorn passed her by without notice.

The afternoon was already advanced. She had meant to set out early but the Duke had been kindness itself. Sweet, sensuous kisses, dainty foods, solicitous affections. She was not deceived. A line had been drawn under their account, a final termination made. Isobel sensed that this master of indecision was clearing the decks for some new development. What might that be?

As the coach sped down the brae into Queensferry, she drew the blind. She could feel the setts grumbling beneath the wheels as the coachman manoeuvred along the sea port's busy high street. The voices of fishwives, vendors and merchants came in with the salt tang smell of the sea.

Whatever Hamilton intended, she was not included in his plans. What else had she expected? In truth this was the end she had foreseen, when, with Nellie's encouragement, the liaison had been renewed. An honourable settlement that was also a conclusion.

Was the Duke planning a rebellion or a capitulation? Would he at last bid for the crown that he so dearly believed was his due? Isobel was doubtful; so much resolution seemed out of character. Yet some options were definitely being ruled in or out. Her own rounding off was certainly satisfactory or, as Nellie would claim, advantageous, but something in her own heart and soul was being shut down. Was that how people recognised love, retrospectively and with regret?

From the moment the coach entered Leith, progress

slowed dramatically. Everywhere seemed noisily packed with traffic and crowds of onlookers going nowhere in particular. In an attempt to bypass the jams, the coachman re-routed by Bonnington Mill and Pilrig. But it was still another hour before they were approaching the Netherbow, reduced to a crawl by queues trying to enter and leave by the old Port.

Daniel would have it demolished to improve the flow of carts and coaches, thought Isobel wryly. Yet this crowd felt more political than commercial. The Netherbow was one of Edinburgh's finest buildings, towered, spired and repeatedly ornamented in honour of the nation's absent kings. For years she had lived in its shadow, beneath the ringing of its bell in ceremony, curfew, alarm, celebration and grief. As the carriage edged through, the bell struck six hours. Would it toll or peal if Parliament voted for Union?

Isobel found herself looking forward to the snug parlour, so intimate and warm after the cold grandeur of Kinneil. A picture of Foe relaxing by the hearth came unbidden to her mind. She had told him little and he had not pried. In his own way Daniel Foe, merchant of London, was a true gentleman.

The coach came to a halt. She could hear the panting of the two hard-worked horses as the door opened halfway. Quickly she stepped out and up the stairs. Her bags were dumped unceremoniously behind her on the landing. She did not look back but with a burst of anticipation pushed open the door of her own small refuge.

'Welcome home.'

Catherine sat by the fire, divested of hat and cloak. She was ensconced, Isobel observed sharply, in her own chair, and Daniel's seat was empty.

'I did not expect you.'

'I returned early from Ireland. Mr Foe acted host, not knowing when you would be back.'

'I was in the country on business. Mr Foe is very settled here.'

Isobel drew off her gloves and cloak and untied her hat, maintaining a careful composure, aware of Catherine watching her closely.

'Did you see the Duke?' For all her apparent self-possession, Catherine was unable to restrain a nervous desire for information.

'The Duke? I am not involved in public affairs, as you know better than any.'

'Forgive me, I'm too abrupt.'

'Why are you back?' Isobel sat down on the settle.

Catherine abandoned caution and pretence. She had no further reserves to fall back on and the sight of a known face unlocked her pent up feelings. 'Things are at a crisis.'

'What do you mean?' interrogated Isobel, unyielding.

'The Union will be stopped.'

'Parliament is set to confirm it, as every cadie on the High Street could tell you.'

'On the day the Act is passed, the peers and burghs will leave Parliament in protest. That is the signal for revolt and North and South will rise together.'

'Jacobites and Covenanters? How do you know that?'

'There are men of honour even among the sectarians, and able soldiers.'

Isobel could feel her stomach shifting but she held stiffly on to the carved arm. 'You don't meet them in society.' She had not steered a difficult course to be shipwrecked now. 'I don't want to know anything about this, Catherine. Tomorrow you must leave my house and not come back.'

'You don't support Scotland's cause.' The voice trembled despite itself.

'I don't support or oppose any king.' Isobel's tone was flat and emotionless. 'That would be to reach beyond my place and yours.'

'You could be a duchess,' Catherine flared up.

'You know nothing about it.'

'Why pay court to what pushes you down? I'm at least willing to fight for my own cause.' Catherine was on her feet, at her full, magnificent height.

'That's because you have nothing to lose.' Isobel remained seated and rigidly under control. 'You can stay here tonight but early tomorrow I want you away for good.'

'Is that your last word?'

She would not meet Catherine's accusing stare, yet there was a fraction of a second of silence before she mastered the word. 'Yes.'

'Then I shall leave this evening.'

'As you please.'

Catherine swung out and up the stairs to her old room.

৯৯৯

Though it was not yet fully dark, the shutters were closed

and two candles burned on the window ledge. Foe sat on a stool, his back to the window, clutching a sheaf of papers.

'The City of Glasgow has obtained a character for their bold profession of truth, under the fury of Popish and Episcopal government.' Despite his subdued tones, Foe tried to breathe some life into the text. 'But what now? Look about you! What company do you keep? Presbyterians leagued with Jacobites. Papists on your right hand, the French at your back.'

Rhetorical whispering did no justice to the task. Foe threw the bundle of papers carelessly onto his bed. His mind moved back to the scene earlier that evening in the parlour. Had he been too forthcoming? Without promising anything specific, had he suggested the possibility of more assistance than he could actually offer? Beneath the raven deeps of her hair, the pupils of her dark eyes had seemed strangely dilated.

There was a gentle tap on the door. Foe drew the bolt and opened it to reveal Lady Catherine's strained yet luminous face. 'Can I come in?' She spoke in a whispered undertone.

'Lady –'

'Please keep your voice low. I do not want Mrs Rankin to hear.'

A little dazed, Foe stepped back and gestured her into his sanctuary. She sat down on the bed. Foe noticed that without wig or hat, her own hair was loosening below each ear.

'What's the matter?' He remained standing near the door, which he had pushed to.

'Mrs Rankin will not allow me to stay.'

'Have you quarrelled?'

'She thinks it is too dangerous.'

'Dangerous?'

'I need to throw myself on your mercy.'

'What could I do?'

'Tonight I have to meet with a man in whom I cannot place any trust.'

'Why put yourself at risk?'

Catherine looked towards the vacant stool, and taking the hint Foe crossed in front of her and sat down. The moment of unguarded surprise had gone; and his mind raced with possibilities.

'You support the Union,' Catherine began, 'but many of my friends in Ireland oppose it. I have been charged with passing on some information secretly.'

'Jacobite dispatches. You could be charged with treason and hanged.'

'I have no choice for reasons I cannot explain. When I hand over this package my value is at an end. I have no-one to protect me.'

'I will follow you.'

'I cannot ask such a thing, but if you could wait nearby and see me safely away from this assignation...'

'You are without husband or father. This has been the cause of your trouble. I will stay close and see that you come to no harm.'

'Even Isobel has abandoned me.'

'She has to consider her own situation. Will you then be free of this whole business?'

'Yes. I know I have no right to ask this service.'

'Yours are the claims of mercy and not of justice. You are alone and friendless.'

'You are a good man, Mr Foe, and I thank you with all my heart.'

Catherine had come to her feet. With one swift movement she closed the gap between them, pressed both his hands in hers, and then withdrew. 'You might put yourself in danger. Have you a sword?'

'God forgive me, I once killed a man in a duel. I swore never to draw my sword again in anger but I still know how to use it.'

'I must be above the Tron in about three hours, after curfew. My meeting is in Warriston Close. Keep to the other side of the street until you see me come out.'

Foe sensed the calculation beneath her anxiety. 'You can depend on it.'

'Thank you.' With that, she was through the door and away.

Foe pressed the bolt gently home and turned back into the room. The papers still lay scattered, open to view. The article would have to do as it was. A vital connection had been here all along in this house, before his own eyes.

കൈകൈ

Ten minutes after her interview with Foe, Catherine was

on the High Street again, cloaked and hatted. She made no attempt to conceal her exit since she knew of old that everything on the stair was heard and marked. She had washed and her hair was neatly tied back. Amidst the gathering shadows, she slipped through the Netherbow Port and into the Canongate.

Over these last days she had not paused to consider or reflect. Her every action was driven by the desire to complete the mission on which she and Aeneas had embarked. Each next move had seemed clear and right, the product of nerves fine-tuned by fear and determination. The long term consequences were of no concern or relevance to Catherine's instinctive urge to succeed and survive.

The Canongate was full of cadies, carriages and horsemen. She kept off the causeway, avoiding torches and lanterns, till she found Glamis' mansion. In the atmosphere of bustle and anticipation, it was shrouded in silence and darkness behind its high walls.

This was where Aeneas had lived, and then lost the battle with his former patron. A stab of longing passed through her as she thought of the slim body on which Glamis had preyed. But she held herself against the emotion and moved forward to the gates. Within minutes she was being ushered into the Earl's private apartments.

He was unchanged, formally dressed, even at home. He held her at a distance with a long calculating stare. 'I had your note at Parliament, and tore myself away from affairs of state. You found my lodgings.'

'I had to speak with you today.'

'Don't distress yourself, my dear. I have missed you immensely. I repeatedly asked the good Mistress Rankin where you had flown off to, but she could not or would not assist.' He moved forward to remove her cloak. 'No matter, now you have returned with your charms intact.'

'I have been in France.'

Glamis took an involuntary step back. The ironical green eyes focused on her face. 'France?'

'At the Court.'

'The devil you have.'

'I have been sent to ask why no message has been received from you. No sign or signal.'

'Treason's no game for a woman.' The thin lips curved in disdain.

'My presence here is totally discreet.'

'I wouldn't say as much.'

'Are you ready to act?'

'Would you interrogate me?'

'I am only the messenger.'

'Then confine yourself to that, and other more opportune functions.' An arm gestured towards the bedchamber but Glamis' mind was clearly elsewhere.

'We must be assured of your intentions.'

'We. How quaint. I could have you arrested tonight. Were I not so devoted.' He seemed dangerously sure of his ground.

'I'm not here for pleasure.'

'No? Then let me confer some.' He made a grab for her arm.

'I must go.'

'Not before we renew acquaintance.'

Her arm was firmly caught and he pulled at her cloak with his free hand. Catherine moved towards him to relieve the pressure, and then jerked a well-aimed knee into the oncoming lower body. Glamis doubled, muffling a cry of agony.

'Is that familiar enough for you?' She struck again as he fell groaning on the floor.

'I'll see you stripped and hung out,' he hissed in pain, but he did not call for help.

'I'll play the man's part then, since you refuse, or perhaps you're not able.'

'You're mad, whore. You'll not escape.'

Clutching the cloak around her trembling body, Catherine left, forcing herself to move slowly past the servants and household guards. As she emerged into the evening cool of the Canongate, she increased her pace. As she had expected, there was no help to be found in Glamis. She was now completely alone, apart from her desperate gamble on Foe's protection.

 তততত

'Excuse me, Isobel.' Foe had knocked gently on the parlour

door.

'Are you alright?'

'Yes, fine. Just a little unsettled tonight.'

'Come in and sit down,' she urged cordially. 'Everything is uneasy tonight. You can hear it in the streets.'

'That is why I must speak with you.' Foe was now positioned by the fire, ready for confidences.

'I am glad of that, since I need to speak to you as well.'

'What's wrong?' Intent on his own confession, Foe was caught off guard.

'Forgive me for being direct.' Isobel adopted a firm tone. 'We have grown used to each other, Daniel. I know that you are sympathetic to the Protestant cause and I have read your efforts to persuade opinion. But have you had any contact with the Covenanters?'

'I have been in communication indirectly with the Covenanting party,' replied Foe cautiously. But Isobel Rankin was not to be deflected.

'Do you know Colonel Kennedy of Ballintrae?'

'He gives tuition in fencing. Why do you ask?'

'You have had lessons from Colonel Kennedy, have you not?'

'He is an honourable soldier.' Where was this leading? Foe's thoughts whirled, seeking a fixed landing without success.

'That's as may be. He could be playing a game that puts you at risk.'

'What have you heard?'

'I've been turning this over in my mind all evening. I can't tell you the source of my information, but I can tell you that Lady O'Kelly is not what she seems.'

Foe managed to marshall his wits. This was to be a

night of revelations. 'You hinted at that before. Her secret is safe with me.'

This is much more serious,' Isobel brushed aside his caution and her own reserve. 'Make no rash pledges, Daniel. Her widowhood is a convenient fiction. She has come by way of Ireland with messages from the Jacobite Court.'

'For the opposition.'

'And for the Covenanters.'

'The Covenanters.' Foe was up and pacing. 'You mean for Kennedy.' He turned round at speed. 'Of course! He's the only one in Edinburgh who can speak for the sectarians. How could I have been so short-sighted? You may have saved me from a terrible mistake.'

'What do you mean?' This was more than Isobel had expected. 'Remember, I am not the source of your suspicions.'

'I would take your confidence to the grave.' Foe had grasped both her hands.

'How deeply are you involved in this?' pressed Isobel, her composure rattled. 'I thought you were a merchant, not a plotter.'

'I have the trust of the best men in Scotland,' Foe said proudly.

'Rely only on yourself. Listen.' They both froze, hearing a light footfall on the stair. 'She's come back to collect her things and then leave for good.'

Releasing her hands, Foe stood like a soldier ready for duty. 'I must follow her.'

'Why?'

'She may put us both in danger.' A look passed between them.

'If you leave your door ajar and snuff out the candle

you can hear any stirring on the stair. Is it worth the risk?' counselled Isobel.

'This may be the best chance fortune has ever dealt me. To prevent a rebellion is to please the most powerful patrons.'

'For God's sake, be careful. Kennedy is a violent and ruthless man.' Isobel was at the doorway, looking up the stair.

'Is she in her room now?'

'Yes.'

'Then I'll go and get ready. Will you wait up?'

'I'll be here by the fire.' She seemed a small and irresolute figure, gesturing towards the hearth.

'Don't worry if I am delayed. I'll turn the trail of any trouble elsewhere.' Foe was animated and enlarged by crisis; his solid figure resonated with decision.

'I don't understand, Daniel, but I put my trust in you. Take care. Please be careful.'

'I shall.' He was gone, pulling the door deftly behind him.

જ઼જ઼જ઼

'Edinburgh's a dark city by night.' The voice came from

the murky mouth of Warriston Close, though Catherine had been hovering in its shadows for the last ten minutes and had seen no-one come in or out.

'But the people are hospitable to king and commoner.'

'Step in here. I wasn't expecting you to come back.'

Catherine went down five steps and pushed the package into the outstretched hands. 'These are the numbers and dispositions.' She kept one arm withdrawn.

'Are they all here?' She could hear the rustling of papers.

'A few are still wavering but they'll come in when it begins. All the names you need are there.'

A tinder flared briefly, showing for an instant Kennedy's massive, heavy-browed face in a fiery glow.

'Aye, these are the goods.'

She refused this any response.

'You have a Scots tongue beneath your Irish fashion. Are you known in Edinburgh?'

'Only by another name. I am leaving tomorrow.'

'Don't delay then. Your presence here is a danger to everyone now these are safely delivered.'

'I'll watch out for myself.' Catherine turned for the steps.

'Farewell then, lady.'

'Behind you.' The voice came from deeper in the close.

But it was too late. She felt herself dragged back down and a searing pain sprang up in her side.

'Never trust a woman,' grunted Kennedy with venom, but she had her arm clear and drove her knife heavily into yielding flesh.

A vicious muted struggle followed in the close mouth. Whimpers of desperation masked an animal fury. 'Bastard, you've hurt me.' She clawed desperately up the steps.

Suddenly she felt Kennedy's weight being pulled off.

Stumbling to her feet, half-running and half-staggering, she escaped into the deserted High Street.

'Colonel Kennedy, let me assist you.' Foe was cool and collected in the dark.

'Where the hell did you spring from?'

'Let me move you to shelter.'

'I'm better here.'

'I saw the whole business.'

'Well done.'

'You've played a double hand, Kennedy.'

'Not to you.'

'To my cause and your own.'

Kennedy moaned in pain and frustration. 'We're on the same side, you fool. I'm in the pay of government, the same as you.'

'To split the rebels?'

'They're to be unleashed, man. Draw the poison before it bursts. Like my innards.' He clutched at his bleeding belly.

'Provoke a revolt?' Foe felt it like a sharp blow to the face.

'You've been used, Foe, like everyone else. Now stop gawping and get a quack. The wild cat's just about done for me.'

'I must find her.' Foe started up for the street, abandoning the wounded man.

'She'll have gone to ground somewhere nearby. Finish her off, but get me a surgeon.'

Kennedy's voice was lost down the black depths of Warriston Close.

❧❧❧

'The bleeding's slower. I'll unroll the bandage now.'

Catherine was laid out on the parlour floor in front of the fire. Isobel was on her knees unwinding a cloth bandage. Beside her was a basin full of warm reddening water and a pile of bloody clouts.

'Is it deep?'

'The blood may be the worst of it but I can't really tell.' Isobel kept unwinding.

'I should still leave tonight,' Catherine clutched her nurse's hand till Isobel gently loosened the hold.

'You can't travel, Catherine. I don't know how you got back here without help. Hide for a few days till you regain some strength.'

'If I'm caught now, everything is wasted.'

'What does it matter, compared to life?' chided Isobel.

'My life has no worth to them now. The signal may go by another route, but the alarm must not be raised.'

'Did you kill Kennedy?' Isobel did not recognise this single-minded and potentially ruthless passion.

'I don't think so. Mr Foe came hard on my heels. How did he know what was afoot?'

Neither woman stopped to consider the possible answers. 'I must get away, Isobel, for your sake as well as mine.'

Isobel proceeded to bandage steadily, passing folds gently under the slender waist.

'Calm yourself,' she soothed, 'and look to your own health. The rising will come to nothing.'

'What will you do with me?'

'Nothing, lassie, nothing except what will get you clear. I want you out of this treacherous town. Rebellion cannot succeed if the Duke will not support it.'

'He is to lead the protest.'

'Hush now, lass. Hamilton will risk nothing. Blow hot,

blow cold, do nothing. I should know better than any.'

The bandaging was finished and Catherine sank back on her pillows with relief.

'So it was true.'

'Soon you can go back to Ireland and to safety.'

'I'll wait for Foe. No doubt he can arrange for my arrest.'

'Don't be stupid. We'll get you away to Ireland, to France and to your husband Robert. Go to the Americas or the Indies and start again. You've done it before.'

'Robert is ruined.' This came in a small hard tone of finality and defeat. 'He might as well be dead.'

'Try your luck again. Fortune can always be won back,' she encouraged, tying the loose ends together.

'He's rotten with syphilis. I haven't let him near me for two years. Robert crawls around St Germain slobbering after every chambermaid.'

'Catherine, my poor lamb,' Isobel held the younger woman's face in her hands. 'Then why, why all this?'

'For me, Isobel.' She half-rose on her pillow. 'For me against the world. The gamble and the winning. What's new about that?'

'I'm truly sorry. I thought there was one man on whom you could depend.'

'Like you.'

She lowered Catherine's head gently back against the pillow.

'Whatever it takes, I'll have you in a private coach tonight. You'll need brandy, spare bandages, some food. I know someone in Glasgow who'll keep you for a month. No one will trouble a woman in pain after a stillbirth. Then on to Ayr. Mr Foe will help you to the carriage.'

'Why would he help?'

'For decency and kindness' sake. There is more to Daniel Foe than meets the eye. Now lie back completely.I want another look at this wound.'

The fever of resolve seemed to ebb away for the first time in weeks. A wave of release passed through Catherine's throbbing body as Isobel's small fingers probed gently around the fissure.

'Why would you help me?' Catherine's dark eyes were dilated and staring at Isobel.

'Because I love you. What possessed you to carry a knife?'

'I always had one, even then.'

'I never knew. But it proved its value tonight. This wound was supposed to deliver death. Hold still and I'll bind another bandage round you.'

తతత

'It is a great satisfaction to the Queen that the Union is

happily concluded in her reign. I am commanded by Her Majesty to assure you that she shall do all in her power to make these islands feel the benefits. If the finishing of this great affair is acceptable to you, I shall now proceed to touch the Act with the royal sceptre of Scotland.'

Chancellor Seafield strove to maintain the level tones of normal business, but his calming procedure was interrupted by Glamis, who rose awkwardly to his feet, commanding attention on all sides.

'My Lord, the accumulated protests of this hall have not been enough to stay your hand. The Earl of Atholl has declared the course of this Parliament to be indecent, illegal and irregular. The Earl of Mar has condemned our proceedings as treasonable, even as the twenty-second and last article of the treaty was passed by forty votes, mine included.'

For this final session Foe had an advantageous position near the front of the gallery. Some members had absented themselves from the business, though from a variety of motives.

'But what if,' continued Glamis, 'what if in the moment that the sceptre is lowered the peers and burghs of this realm were to leave in solemn protest? What might be the effect of such an exodus on our inflamed populace? None can reckon. Such, my Lord, is the desperate course of action bandied in the streets. So great the threat that none less than His Grace the Duke of Hamilton would march at its head.' The tensions in the hall were palpable. Was there yet to be a reversal? 'But today the Duke is indisposed. A cold confines him at Kinneil.'

There were neither cheers nor jeers but an unnatural stony silence along the benches and across the gallery. Glamis let the moment of deflation, his moment, sink in slowly.

'The tides of protest,' he resumed, 'must be stayed for now. The Union will go forward with all its opportunities. Yet we are still able to be moved by the fate of our ancient nation. The flame of patriotism is undimmed in my heart at least. We shall remain aroused to see justice done. I thank your Lordship.'

Queensberry rose in turn to acknowledge Glamis and make a short reply. The Chancellor was still immobile at his place of duty.

'Our posterity will reap the profit of Union and I know that as Parliament has the honour to conclude it, you will in your several stations recommend to the people a grateful sense of Her Majesty's goodness and care.' A rising clamour of protest could be heard from beyond the hall's elaborate leaded windows, but Queensberry barely paused to draw breath. 'And that you will promote a universal desire in this kingdom to become one in heart and mind as we are inseparably joined in interest with our neighbour nation.'

He sat down, and the moment could be delayed no longer.

Seafield lifted the ornate silver wand from its place beside the royal crown of Scotland.

'I take the sceptre.'

He lowered it and touched the Act of Union. 'That's the end of an auld sang.'

❧❧❧

When Parliament first voted to negotiate for a Union

the uprising of protest had been spontaneous. This was different; it was organised. As the debate proceeded in the Hall towards its inevitable conclusion, men were moving into the Canongate from Leith and Abbeyhill, and into the Grassmarket from the West Port. They had come from all parts of central Scotland, expecting a capitulation but hoping for revolt. The riots broke out simultaneously on both sides of town. The uproar had been anticipated and the Parliamentary session concluded early so that all the key players could make their escape.

Rather than sign the Treaty at Parliament, Queensberry had arranged for the Scottish Commissioners to meet secretly in the gardens of Moray House, the former town house of the Moray Earls, which boasted extensive grounds sloping down to the Holyrood burn. Access could be gained from the Canongate or by a postern in the lower boundary wall. One by one, the noble Commissioners slipped into the garden and converged on the tiled summerhouse at the foot of the slope.

Though Glamis had not been party to the London negotiations, Queensberry had ensured his presence at this ritual conclusion. The two former antagonists paced the regimented paths waiting for the full complement to assemble. The yells and clash of violent protest could be heard from the main thoroughfare.

'Is your house well protected?' asked Glamis.

'My wife and invalid son are safely guarded at home.' It was rare for the Marquis to mention his lunatic child and heir.

'I have a favour to ask.'

The elusive motion worked beneath Queensberry's flaccid face, signalling full attention.

'There was a Jacobite courier here in Edinburgh, a

young woman.'

'There have been several couriers, my Lord Glamis.' The caution was audible.

'This one has played out her little part.'

'Why then should she concern us further?'

'I have a particular reason, a private reason, for wishing her apprehended.'

'Alive or dead?' Queensberry was direct.

'Dead, by whatever means.'

Queensberry raised a quizzical eyebrow. 'You surprise me, my Lord. However I am profoundly in your debt and more than willing to oblige.' Do you know where this pretty emissary has gone to ground?'

'I regret not. She travelled here from Ireland.'

'I shall make enquiries. Consider the matter closed.'

'Your Lordship, I hope I dare soon say your Grace, is most kind.' Glamis inclined courteously.

'Shall we go in?'

As Queensberry ushered the Commissioners into his cramped stone summerhouse, servants and rioters alike abandoned his town house. His poor son and heir had been left free to roam and was shambling down towards the kitchen. Oblivious to the dramatic events above, a young servant boy was turning a spitted calf over a huge open fire. Not everyone would come through that long night of riotous protest unscathed.

❧❧❧

The Secretary of State sat at a small table in his private

chamber. Two empty claret bottles stood neglected at one side. As Harley sank lower and lower over his labours, the ornately carved back of his chair climbed increasingly into view. Every few minutes Reid brought in another bundle of papers tied with red ribbon. Harley undid the ribbon with deliberate concentration and examined each sheet, transferring them one by one to the other side of the table. Every bundle was then retied by Reid and removed. As the manservant deposited a further unopened bundle, he stood back and waited.

'Is that them all?'

'Aye.'

'All copied.'

'Every one.'

'Good. They may not be needed but you can't be too careful.' Harley patted the last reconstructed bundle reassuringly. 'The complete record of my dealings over this Union affair.'

Under Harley's avid gaze, Reid advanced to tie the last ribbon. 'A Scots rising cannae hairm ye noo.'

'It's my friends, William, not my enemies that I fear. The closer, the more dangerous.' Each word was too precisely placed, but unslurred.

'Shall I fetch anither bottle?'

'No, reach me some of your Scotch spirits.'

Reid disappeared with the last bundle. As he reappeared with a whisky bottle, Harley drew a stray paper from his waistcoat. 'What do you think of this? It's by Daniel Foe.'

Reid drew the cork and proceeded to pour.

'*Union is nature's strong cement*
The life of power and soul of government.
Behold Britannia fitted to command the globe
Her Queen how bright how suited to the robe.

161

With what regret do neighbour nations see
The prospect of this new felicity...
Is that not a fine sentiment?'

'Verra upliftin.'

'But not poetry. Unlike this nectar.' Harley sipped appreciatively.

'There's nae music tae it,' Reid dragged out grudgingly.

'Poor Foe, he has no ear for a Scottish melody. He's, what would you call it?'

'Deaf.'

'Deaf? Well, ears made of cloth anyway. Has he come back to London?'

'No, he's scrievin a history.'

'A discreet one I trust. Did we ever pay him?' Harley continued to sip contentedly.

'No yet.'

'Who can tell, Foe may make his way without our patronage. Write to him tomorrow. His service is over.'

'Verra guid, I'll see tae it. Will ye retire noo?'

'Not yet. Sometimes I sleep better upright. Leave the bottle handy.' A weary hand was hardly raised.

'I'll awa then.'

'Thank you, William. I value your service.' Reid stiffened with displeasure. 'Sometimes I think this Scottish business will live to haunt me.'

'Aye weill, I'll gie you guid nicht.' Reid was gone with his usual quiet tread.

Harley reached for the bottle and poured himself a full tumbler. 'My faithful Scotch, guid nicht.'

కాడకాడకా

As the boat eased its way into the great harbour of

Antwerp, Catherine pulled the cloak tighter around her shoulders to ward off the grey mist which was forming above the sluggish waves. Since land had been sighted she had been glad to stand on deck, leaving behind the stale salty odours of the galley and berths. Lights flickered into life through the dusk on the distant quay across the basin of the Scheldt.

Since leaving Glasgow, Catherine had felt tension and fear rise back within her healing body to possess it once more. Yet the Antwerp docks represented safety and an easy overland journey to St Germain. Behind her lay subterfuge, deception, alarms and narrow escape, but what occupied her emotions was what awaited her at the end of the journey.

Edinburgh had been treacherous yet at the last Isobel had cared for her like a daughter, smuggling her away to Glasgow and the homely if inquisitive attentions of Nellie MacConnochie. In that city Catherine had enjoyed refuge and shelter for nearly two months while the deep flesh wound in her side closed and her strength was recovered. Nellie was a bold, big-boned woman, slightly younger than Isobel. The Glasgow trade, as Catherine had observed from the sidelines, was less refined. Even the wealthy, fuelled by copious quantities of drink, seemed to relish the low life.

Still, she had been left in peace, protected by Isobel Rankin's name and money. From Glasgow she had gone by cart, dressed in her peasant clothes, to take a little boat at Dunure. The Ayrshire coast seemed to be porous with unofficial routes across to Ireland and beyond, out of the control if not the ken of Scotland's leaky customs service. No-one had looked askance at the humble though handsome woman travelling to Belfast to join her husband.

She had made it her business to avert attention just as she knew how to attract it when the need arose.

Ireland, Catherine reflected, had provided the one risky moment in her well-conceived plan of retreat. On leaving the boat in Belfast harbour she had struggled to find a private room in which she could change identity to a respectable lady travelling to Europe. Arriving in one disguise she left in another, and had gone unchallenged.

Catherine's thoughts swung towards her destination. Would Robert be unchanged towards her? Disease must have eaten further into his constitution. What if he had succumbed to the wasting sickness and dissipation? Could she retain her own position at Court? Would she see Aeneas, or had he withdrawn to the seminary? Catherine could feel the strangeness of a new life inside her. She wanted to wrap herself protectively around that fragile plant. This time, whatever happened, she would see a baby grow and have a soft warm mouth sucking at her breasts. Already her nipples were stretching and tense.

Perhaps it was better not to look ahead. These speculations brought with them the fears she struggled to restrain. Instead, she yielded to the languor of the moment as the sloop cut a steady curve through the anchored ships and calm fetid water of the inner port.

ಭ್ಞ–ಭ್ಞ–ಭ್ಞ

Her guard relaxed, Catherine thought Aeneas was waiting

on the quay to meet her. She felt his tall angular frame leaning over to look into her eyes and call her name. That was the trouble with letting go; the mind wandered where it willed. Resolutely she went to check her trunk and bags, which were already lined on deck ready for disembarking. At least the long ordeal of being hunted was finished. No longer need she cower with nerves quivering.

The boat shuddered as it hit the quay. A welter of guttural voices rose on both sides as ropes were thrown and secured, and goods hauled up. Finally the small group of passengers were helped across the narrow walkway onto dry stone. It was odd how Flemish words could leap out from the stream of a sentence in familiar Scots – hoose, kirk, whure.

Messengers and carriers clustered round the knot of arrivals. Two men, an older and a younger, pulled at Catherine's luggage.

'English? English?'

She nodded.

'To inn?'

She pointed to the bags but they were already hoisting them up. 'Goot, to inn.' They moved ahead of her on the quay, the older man shouldering the big trunk with his younger shorter companion carrying the loose bags. Catherine muttered a polite farewell but the other passengers were intent on their own porters and directions.

☙☙☙

The harbourside was crammed with fish stalls, merchant

booths, chandlers and taverns. Men sat in the open air on stools drinking ale from huge jugs and smoking clay pipes. The porters turned down a street off the front and Catherine followed, pleased to escape the leers and comments. She had vague memories of the town square in Antwerp with its spacious inns and high-storeyed guild halls.

The grey-bearded man turned beneath his trunk to beckon her on as they moved along the narrow streets into the dense heart of the city. At one crossroads, her two guides paused as if getting a bearing and then went left into a quieter street with tall timber-galleried houses on each side that almost met above the passage. Then the younger man took a sharp right into a yet smaller alley, while his fellow waited to usher Catherine round.

Suddenly they were in front of a shabby door in a gloomy courtyard. Catherine looked round, 'Ney, ney goot,' she queried, turning towards the street. She did not see her luggage being dumped but she heard a lock turn before a hand was clamped over her mouth and a rough arm dragged her backwards through the doorway. Within seconds she was inside a bare-boarded grubby room and tied to a wooden chair.

While the older man gagged her with a filthy rag, the younger moved swiftly to light half-burnt candles in pewter holders. Then he stooped to rip open her baggage with a knife. She was being mercilessly and efficiently robbed. As her belongings spilled out on the floor, Catherine could see that the only furniture apart from her seat was a straw pallet on the boards.

The red-haired man was slight, but muscular and agile. He was intent on his search. Her small stock of dresses was soon scattered across the floor. A jewellery case was tipped out, with meagre results. The few books she possessed were shaken and tossed aside. At the very foot of the trunk was one early sketch of Catherine made by Aeneas before he embarked on the paintings that she had thrown on the fire. This she had hidden and saved and she moaned incoherently behind the gag as it was unrolled. He did not tear it across. Instead he waved it at the older man.

'See, it's her. I telt you.'

Catherine eyes widened. She was invaded by terror.

'Cut her loose.'

As her hands came free she tried to shove the chair back but the man behind her held it firmly. The knife-point was beneath her chin and she was forced up and across the room. Her breath came rapidly forced through her nostrils, the rhythm broken by suppressed whimpers. She had been hunted down and had fallen into her captors' snare.

'Aye, you have two Scotsmen to welcome you. Did you think you'd win free? What do you say, Sandy? The whure thocht she had got away.'

An arid smile spread across the speaker's freckled face.

Sandy grunted.

'Did you hear me, bitch? Can you no talk?'

Then he felled her with one blow to the face. Tears of pain welled as she lay but her consciousness was dulled by shock. He bent down and ripped her dress, exposing one breast. He drew the knife casually across her nipple. Even as she screamed in agony he was dragging her onto the pallet. She fought back instinctively, through a throbbing red haze. 'Haud her doon till I get another grip.' As weight pressed down on her she felt a dark stabbing pain, a burning tear to her guts. She saw in her line of vision the yellow candle flame shiver in its own wax. Then everything went white. A blank sheet.

❧❧❧

'Excellent, thank you. The gravy – sorry, sauce – was

delicious. The finest tavern in Auld Reekie could not produce its equal.' Foe wiped his juicy mouth fastidiously with Isobel's best linen. 'You are a mistress of the culinary arts.'

'It was a good piece of beef,' she demurred graciously. 'Scots beef?'

'British beef.'

'I drink to that honoured cow.' Foe raised his glass, which was replete with a rich Burgundy wine.

'Your work here must be almost finished, Daniel, now that the Covenanters have dispersed.'

And thank goodness they disbanded without bloodshed. But I have my history to complete.'

'Think of your wife and family.' Isobel sipped her own wine modestly. The two were established comfortably in the parlour. A small table had been set up between the carved settle and the two fireside chairs. Isobel replaced her glass.

'I cannot go home empty handed.'

'Daniel Foe, pamphleteer turned scholar. You have as many colours as the rainbow.'

'Who else knows as much about this tale as I do?' parried Foe. 'Do I not have a duty to turn author?'

'You have the information but is it wise to publicise your knowledge?' she queried.

'Matters of state demand privacy, but this will be a public, not a secret, history.'

Isobel seized on this admission. 'Then it cannot tell the whole story.'

'You need actors to reveal the power of secret motives.' Foe acknowledged the force of her point yet sought to divert it. 'Players for intrigue. But their aim is to please through immorality. They corrupt the public taste; my history will improve public understanding.'

'Surely the players act out what people do – hold a mirror up to life.'

'Theatre people act to please the crowd.'

'I can't argue with you,' laughed Isobel, 'for I've only been in a theatre twice in my life. Edinburgh doesn't have one. Perhaps the playhouse will be a blessing of the Union.'

'God forbid,' Foe swallowed the bait, 'The pits and boxes glitter with fops, masked beauties and old sinners. The galleries are packed with pimps, pickpockets and cheap whores.'

'Then reform the playhouse, Daniel!'

'You'd have to knock it down first,' admonished Foe. 'We must stay with history. Otherwise characters who should be kept in the wings will force themselves onto the stage.'

'Discretion must prevail,' yielded Isobel, looking straight across the hearth.

They reflected quietly for a moment.

'You could write a private memoir,' Isobel resumed.

'A confession locked in a vault?'

'What if it were a story in a different voice, as if told by another?'

'The lives of thieves and murderers are told this way in the penny press,' Foe conceded.

'And make for a good sale,' Isobel trumped.

He got up to pace across the small room. 'I might tell the story of an emissary. This man is thrown into prison for his convictions. Debts accumulate, his family is left defenceless, creditors clamour for blood. A powerful man saves him and puts him under an obligation.'

'He becomes the master's spy.'

'His eyes and ears.' Foe resumed his seat, leaning like a storyteller across the hearth. 'Then one day the great man summons him and sends him out like Abraham, he knows not where, he barely knows why. In a neighbouring country, he communicates with Government and Court. He influences the Church and the landed man. He negotiates with merchants and pleads the cause of honest traders. And all the time his pen is busy confiding, reporting and persuading.'

The story had come close to home.

'Is his master pleased?'

Foe sighed. 'The great man receives intelligence but gives none.'

'The emissary is alone. How does the story end?'

'The great man may betray his servant, or cast him off. His usefulness is over.'

'But his silence is still important,' Isobel prompted. 'The great man may be waiting till he needs his emissary again.'

'So the memoir is unfinished and cannot be published.' Foe sank back into his seat.

'Perhaps I can provide another?'

'Who is the subject?' Foe warmed immediately to this new twist in the game.

'A woman born with talents and with beauty.'

'As so many are,' he complimented gracefully.

'You're gallant. And justly, for this woman was also handsome. But she lacked the two things necessary – wealth and position.' Foe's shoulders went heavenward. 'She attracts the notice of a man of rank and becomes his mistress. He honours and loves her, but is already married to his fortune and standing.'

'Then she loses her virtue and gains no security,'

observed Foe soberly.

'But she knew that from the beginning. She accepts the great man's gifts and plans her own way in the world.'

'How can she manage alone?'

'The bargain she has struck can be repeated and other women may benefit from her experience.'

'She has found a means of trade.'

'A profitable commerce.'

'But she cannot be accepted in society,' he protested.

'Those who need her services protect her – her clients are men of wealth and privilege.

'Yet her own heart must remain inviolate.'

'Like the emissary, she is alone,' Foe pondered. 'Has this tale a moral?'

'Must memoirs have a moral?' Isobel questioned.

'All art should display virtue and discourage vice.'

'Yet an author must come to a private accommodation or lose the reader's sympathy,' countered Isobel shrewdly.

In a sudden fit of candour Foe abandoned his line of argument. 'Do we want such intimacy? Can we bear the truth of other lives?' He looked openly across the fire.

'Perhaps if we reach an understanding.'

'Like our two nations,' laughed Foe, 'we can be tolerably cordial.'

Isobel stood and taking Foe's deft, busy hands, she raised him to his feet.

'What do they hope for, Daniel?'

'Peace and trade?' Gently he released his right hand and moulded it round her left breast. 'What else?'

'Ever closer union?'

☙☙☙

It is with sincere regret that I left Edinburgh. My feelings for the capital of North Britain had stolen up on me through these months of turmoil, and then fully possessed my affections. But the time for return had come. My faithful spouse and our seven dear children could no longer depend on my father-in-law's generous support.

I was not returning empty-handed, though direct reward for my services was still unforthcoming. I had survived through my own industry, by the pen and not by the sword. There is a lesson the Scots have yet to learn. Perhaps their precipitous city will one day become a place of print and of ideas, like London.

Isobel has given me an idea though I cannot yet discern its whole import. Truth in fiction; lies that contrariwise reveal the inner nature of our lives. To see other people as God sees us, through our deceits and deceptions. Would that I could manage such a task, for I believe that many might purchase these revelations at an attractive price. Eventually I trust that this memoir, unfinished as it is, may find a printer, a middleman to tempt his unwary clients.

Will I ever see her again? It wrenches my heart to leave. But my mind races on like the wheels of a coach. A new world in the making, and devil take the hindmost.

A Long Stride Shortens the Road

Donald Smith

ISBN 1 84282 073 7 PBK £8.99

Ranging from a celebration of the Holyrood parliament to a dialogue between Jamie Saxt and a skull, from a proposed national anthem to an autobiographical journey through pre-history, *A Long Stride Shortens the Road* traverses a Scotland that is irrevocably independent of spirit, yet universal in outlook.

The poetry in this collection charts the main staging posts in Scotland's recent history. As writer, theatre director, storyteller and political foot soldier, Donald Smith has been at the centre of the cultural action. The poems, however, also reveal a personal narrative of exile and attachment, an intimate engagement with Scottish landscape, and a sense of the spiritual in all things.

This book is for anyone interested in the crucible out of which Scotland emerged, and where it might be going. Donald Smith writes poems to reflect on in the early days of a new nation.

A Long Stride Shortens the Road *is a book of poetry that manages to be both intensely Scottish and optimistic.*

THE SCOTSMAN

Caledonia's Last Stand: in search of the lost Scots of Darien

Nat Edwards

ISBN 1 905222 84 X PBK £12.99

History alone could not explain the colony's disastrous outcome; you really had to stand on the shore of Punta Escoces to realise that the Scots were bound to disaster the moment they chose the site of the settlement they christened Caledonia. The bay was a beautiful, deadly trap. NAT EDWARDS

On 2 November 1698 a fleet landed in the Isthmus of Darien to create a colony and launch a new Scottish trading empire. The venture failed dramatically, with a catastrophic loss of life and money, and led to the eventual end of Scottish independence and the beginning of the UK.

Nat Edwards' erratic odyssey to find the graves of the Scots settlers is a reflection of the story of the Scots Company itself, interweaving pirates, street riots, treasure hunters, indigenous peoples and killer bees with the astonishing facts of Darien. Panama is the real-life setting for an almost unbelievable 17th century of Scottish hope and adventure, and Nat Edwards' discoveries are often frustrating, occasionally freakish, but always fascinating.

a startling new theory... THE OBSERVER

Edward's writing, while respecting of the ill-fated colonists, is warm and witty, making the journey through mordern day Panama a vivid and enjoyable one. He paints a picture of a small yet formidable country and the unique culture and customs of its native people. With pirates, lost cities and killer bees to boot, this is at times a surprisingly exciting read.

THE SKINNY

The Price of Scotland: Darien, Union and the Wealth of Nations

Douglas Watt

ISBN 1 906307 09 1 PBK £8.99

The catastrophic failure of the Company of Scotland to establish a colony at Darien in Central America is one of the best known episodes in late 17th century Scottish history. The effort resulted in significant loss of life and money, and was a key issue in the negotiations that led to the Union of 1707.

What led so many Scots to invest such a vast part of the nation's wealth in one company in 1696?

Why did a relatively poor nation think it could take on the powers of the day in world trade?

What was 'The Price of Scotland'?

In this powerful and insightful study of the Company of Scotland, Douglas Watt offers a new perspective on the events that led to the creation of the United Kingdom.

Exceptionally well-written, it reads like a novel... if you're not Scottish and live here – read it. If you're Scottish read it anyway. It's a very, very good book. MATTHEW PERREN

...a compelling and insightful contribution to our understanding of Darien. Bill Jamieson, THE SCOTSMAN

Scotland was a mess in 1700... it is this mess to which Douglas Watt has brought an economist's eye and a poet's sensibility. THE OBSERVER

The Fundamentals of New Caledonia

David Nicol

ISBN 0 946487 93 6 HBK £16.99

This is the tale of ane lyar and and misrepresenter of persones – a time traveller carrying little more that a few half-remembered science fiction yarns for guidance.

Press-ganged by the late 17th century Company of Scotland, he embarks on the ill-destined venture that set out create a New Caledonia, and came to be known as the Darien disaster.

Their tropical colony was projected to build a trading emporium at the heart of Europe's colonial expansion. But in a short time the ambition of Scotland's merchant class was ruined.

In this feverishly written journal, the would-be settlers must adapt to a new world that crumbles about them even as it is being invented.

Apprenticed to a ship surgeon, the narrator faces an eternal conundrum of time travel. Is it reasonable, or fair, to try and alter the course of history?

Only by confronting the powerful can he begin to understand this world. Only by applying his singular insight can he begin to diagnose the settler's plight. And only by embarking on his own personal odyssey can be find remedy.

The Company of Scotland was established by an Act of Parliament. It planned a colony that would announce itself in a founding declaration, and govern itself by a set of rules and ordinances.

These were the founding principles of a new society. Together with basic ideas and practices in economics, politics, religion, medicine, navigation and law, these principles were tested to destruction.

They are presented here as *The Fundamentals of New Caledonia* – an historical fiction of a new world.

The Strange Case of RL Stevenson

Richard Woodhead

ISBN 0 946487 86 3 HBK £16.99

Now understand my state: I am really an invalid, but of a mysterious order. I might be a malade imaginaire, but for one too tangible symptom, my tendency to bleed from the lungs...If you are very nervous, you must recollect a bad haemorrage is always on the cards, with its concomitants of anxiety and horror for those who are beside me. Do you blench?

ROBERT LOUIS STEVENSON, 1886

A consultant physician for 22 years with a strong interest in Robert Louis Stevenson's life and work, Richard Woodhead was intrigued by the questions raised by the references to his symptoms. The assumption that he suffered from consumption – the diagnosis of the day – is challenged here. Consumption (tuberculosis), a scourge of 19th century society, was regarded as severely debilitating if not a death sentence. Dr Woodhead examines how Stevenson's life was affected by his illness and his perception of it.

This fictional work puts words into the mouths of five doctors who treated RLS at different periods of his adult life. Though these doctors existed in real-life, little is documented of their private conversations with RLS. However everything Dr Woodhead postulates could have occurred within the known framework of RLS's life. Detailed use of Stevenson's own writing adds authenticity to the views espoused in the book.

RLS's writing continues to compel readers today. The fact that he did much of his writing while confined to his sickbed is fascinating. What illness could have contributed to his creativity?

The Underground City, a novel set in Scotland

Jules Verne

ISBN 1 84282 080 X

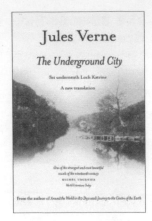

Ten years after he left the exhausted Aberfoyle mine underneath Loch Katrine, the former manger – James Starr – receives an intriguing letter from the old overman – Simon Ford. It suggests that the mine isn't actually barren after all. Despite also receiving an anonymous letter the same day contradicting this, James returns to Aberfoyle and discovers that there is indeed more coal left in the mine to be excavated. However, they are beset by strange events, hinting at a presence that does not wish to see them mine the cave further. Firstly, a stone is thrown at James, but there doesn't seem to have been anyone there. Then, the leaking gas proving that the new mine exists is covered up, and finally James, Simon, and his family are trapped within the new mine as someone, or something, mysteriously blocks up the entrance which they had blown open.

Could it be a person out to sabotage their work? Someone with a grudge against them? Or could it be something supernatural, something they cannot see or understand?

This is a new translation of Jules Verne's novel set underneath Loch Katrine.

Verne is delighting in these details, the science, mythology and geography of the place. Most of Verne's books went through some kind of treatment: some were seen as anti-English, and these parts were taken out, while sometimes one third disappeared.

SUNDAY HERALD

The Bannockburn Years

William Scott

ISBN 0 946487 34 0 PBK £7.95

This is a love story, set at the time of
Scotland's greatest success.

- How did the Scots win the War of
  Independence, against a neighbour 10
  times as powerful?
- Did the Scots have a secret weapon at
  their disposal?
- Was the involvement of women a deciding factor? Should
  Scotland now become independent?

These questions lie at the heart of the medieval manuscript by John
Bannatyne of Bute, genius, commander of the Scottish archers at
Bannockburn, and eye-witness of Robert Bruce's heroic leadership.
A present-day solicitor is asked to stand for the independence party
in an election. In a client's will, he stumbles across reference to a
manuscript of value to the Nation State of Scotland which he tracks
down to the Island of Bute.

Is the document authentic? In the course of his investigation, involving
a World War II fighter pilot, the solicitor also discovers his answer to
the question: should Scotland be independent now?

Written with pace and passion, William Scott has devised an original
vehicle for looking at the future of Scotland. He presents, for the first
time, a convincing explanation of how the victory at Bannockburn was
achieved, with a rigorous examination of the history as part of
the story.

Winner of the 1997 Constable Trophy, the premier award in Scotland
for an unpublished novel, this book offers new insights to both the
general and academic reader, sure to provoke further discussion and
debate.

The story is told with such pace and imagination that it is a compulsive read.
THE SCOTSMAN

A brilliant storyteller. I shall expect to see your name writ large hereafter.
NIGEL TRANTER

Writing in the Sand

Angus Dunn

ISBN 1 905222 91 2 PBK £8.99

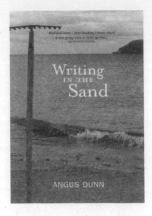

The future hangs on the fall of the sand grains. And time is running out...

On the tip of the Dark Isle lies the tranquil fishing village of Cromness, where the normal round of domino matches, meetings of the Ladies' Guild and twice-daily netting of salmon continues as it always has done. But all is not well.

Down on the beach, and old man rakes the sand, looking for clues to the future. The patterns show him the harmony of the universe, but they also show that there is something wrong in Cromness. Strange things are beginning to happen.

Because this is no ordinary island. Centuries ago, so it is said, the Celtic gods and goddesses took refuge here. Now, behind the walls of the world, there are restless stirring sounds.

As the islanders prepare to celebrate the famed Dark Isle Show, the moment of truth approaches. But is anyone truly aware of the scale of events? And who will prevail?

A fantastic book in every sense of the word.
SCOTS MAGAZINE

It is a latter day baggy monster of a novel... a hallucinogenic soap... the humour at first has shades of Last of the Summer Wine, alternating with the Goons before going all out for the Monty Python meets James Bond, and don't-scrimp-on-the-turbo-charger method... You'll have gathered by now that this book is a grand read. It's an entertainment. It alternates between compassionate and skilful observations, elegantly expressed and rollercoaster abandonment to a mad narrative.
NORTHWORDS NOW

Letters from the Great Wall

Jenni Daiches

ISBN 1 905222 51 3 PBK £9.99

You can't run away from things here in China, there's too much confronting you.

Eleanor Dickinson needs to see things differently. To most her life would seem ideal; 33 years old, a professional university lecturer in a respectable relationship with a man who is keen to start a family. But Eleanor is dissatisfied: she's suffocated by her family and frustrated by the man she has no desire to marry. She has to escape.

In the summer of 1989, she cuts all ties and leaves behind the safe familiarity of Edinburgh to lecture in the eastern strangeness of China, a country on the brink of crisis. Basing herself in Beijing, she sets off on an intense voyage of self-discovery. But as the young democracy movement flexes its muscles, Eleanor is soon drawn into the unfolding drama of an event that captured the world's attention.

What freedoms will be asserted in this ancient nation, shaped both by tradition and revolution? And will Eleanor discover what really matters in her life before the tanks roll into Tiananmen Square?

The Blue Moon Book

Anne MacLeod

ISBN 1 84282 061 3 PBK £9.99

Love can leave you breathless, lost for words.

Jess Kavanagh knows. Doesn't know. 24 hours after meeting and falling for archaeologist and Pictish expert Michael Hurt she suffers a horrific accident that leaves her with aphasia and amnesia. No words. No memory of love.

Michael travels south, unknowing. It is her estranged partner sports journalist Dan McKie who is at the bedside when Jess finally regains consciousness. Dan, forced to review their shared past, is disconcerted by Jess's fear of him, by her loss of memory, loss of words.

Will their relationship survive this test? Should it survive? Will Michael find Jess again? In this absorbing contemporary novel, Anne MacLeod interweaves themes of language, love and loss in patterns as intricate, as haunting as the Pictish Stones.

High on drama and pathos, woven through with fine detail
THE HERALD

As a challenge to romantic fiction, the novel is a success; and as far as men and women's failure to communicate is concerned, it hits the mark.
SCOTLAND ON SUNDAY

100 Favourite Scottish Poems

Edited by Stewart Conn

ISBN 1 905222 61 0 PBK £7.99

Poems to make you laugh. Poems to make you cry. Poems to make you think. Poems to savour. Poems to read out loud. To read again, and again. Scottish poems. Old favourites. New favourites. 100 of the best.

Scotland has a long history of producing outstanding poetry. From the humblest but-and-ben to the grandest castle, the nation has a great tradition of celebration and commemoration through poetry. 100 Favourite Scottish Poems – incorporating the top 20 best-loved poems as selected by a BBC Radio Scotland listener poll – ranges from ballads to Burns, from 'Proud Maisie' to 'The Queen of Sheba', and from 'Cuddle Doon' to 'The Jeelie Piece Song'.

Both wit and wisdom, and that fusion of the two which can touch the heart as well as the mind, distinguishes the work selected by Stewart Conn for his anthology 100 Favourite Scottish Poems *(Luath Press and Scottish Poetry Library, £7.99). This lovely little book ranges from Dunbar to Douglas Dunn, taking in just about all the major and most of the minor Scottish poets of the centuries by means of their most memorable writing.*

THE SCOTSMAN

A Passion for Scotland

David R. Ross

ISBN 1 84282 019 2 PBK £9.99

Eschewing xenophobia, his deep understanding of how Scotland's history touches her people shines through. All over Scotland, into England and Europe, over to Canada, Chicago and Washington – the people and the places that bring Scotland's story to life, and death – including

- Wallace and Bruce
- The Union Montrose
- The Jacobites
- John MacLean
- Tartan Day USA

and, revealed for the first time, the burial places of all Scotland's monarchs.

This is not a history book. But it covers history.

This is not a travel guide. But some places mentioned might be worth a visit.

This is not a political manifesto. But a personal one.

Read this book. It might make you angry. It might give you hope. You might shed a tear. You might not agree with David R. Ross.

But read this book. You might rediscover your roots, your passion for Scotland.

Reportage Scotland: History in the Making

Louise Yeoman
Foreword by Professor David Stevenson
ISBN 1 84282 051 6 PBK £6.99

Events – both major and minor – as seen and recorded by Scots throughout history.

• Which king was murdered in a sewer? What was Dr Fian's love magic?

• Who was the half-roasted abbot?

• Which cardinal was salted and put in a barrel?

• Why did Lord Kitchener's niece try to blow up Burns's cottage?

The answers can all be found in the eclectic mix covering nearly 2000 years of Scottish history. Historian Louise Yeoman's rummage through the manuscript, book and news-papers archives of the National Library of Scotland has yielded an astonishing amount of material. Ranging from a letter to the King of the Picts to Mary Queen of Scots' own account of the murder of David Riccio; from the execution of William Wallace to accounts of anti-poll tax actions and the open-ing of the new Scottish Parliament. The book takes pieces from the original French, Latin, Gaelic and Scots and makes them accessible to the general reader, often for the first time.

Sun Behind the Castle: Edinburgh Poems

Angus Calder
ISBN 1 84282 078 8 PBK £8.99

The Edinburgh of Angus Calder's poems is not the city of summer tourism and landmark buildings. It is the all the year round arena of lingering mists or brilliant sunlight on grey stone, where seagulls and pigeons command the early-morning streets, curlers sweep their ice at Murrayfield and coarse sportsmen revel on the Meadows. World famous Sandy Bell's is not the only pub evoked, and Bread Street features more strongly than Princes Street. This is because the centre of Calder's Edinburgh is Tollcross, terrain of theatres and cheap shops, ethnic restaurants and lapdance bars, just southwest of respectability. The culminating sequence of *Sun Behind the Castle* transports to Tollcross the ancient Roman poet Horace, modernising completely more than a score of his famous Odes, with their gossip and lyricism, fatalism, political comment and hedonistic moralising. 'Carpe diem. Enjoy this delicious biscuit.'

It was once said of Joyce's Ulysses that if Dublin was destroyed, it could be rebuilt as it was by reading the book that memorialised it. Sun Behind the Castle *catalogues Edinburgh with a similar love and energy.*

SUNDAY HERALD

Luath Press Limited

committed to publishing well written books worth reading

LUATH PRESS takes its name from Robert Burns, whose little collie Luath (Gael., swift or nimble) tripped up Jean Armour at a wedding and gave him the chance to speak to the woman who was to be his wife and the abiding love of his life. Burns called one of The Twa Dogs Luath after Cuchullin's hunting dog in *Ossian's Fingal*. Luath Press was established in 1981 in the heart of Burns country, and is now based a few steps up the road from Burns' first lodgings on Edinburgh's Royal Mile.

Luath offers you distinctive writing with a hint of unexpected pleasures.

Most bookshops in the UK, the US, Canada, Australia, New Zealand and parts of Europe, either carry our books in stock or can order them for you. To order direct from us, please send a £sterling cheque, postal order, international money order or your credit card details (number, address of cardholder and expiry date) to us at the address below. Please add post and packing as follows: UK – £1.00 per delivery address; overseas surface mail – £2.50 per delivery address; overseas airmail – £3.50 for the first book to each delivery address, plus £1.00 for each additional book by airmail to the same address. If your order is a gift, we will happily enclose your card or message at no extra charge.

Luath Press Limited
543/2 Castlehill
The Royal Mile
Edinburgh EH1 2ND
Scotland
Telephone: 0131 225 4326 (24 hours)
Fax: 0131 225 4324
email: sales@luath. co.uk
Website: www. luath.co.uk